SOME LIKE IT SECRET

GOING ROYAL
BOOK FOUR

HEATHER LONG

Some Like It Secret/Heather Long – 2nd ed.

ISBN: 978-1-966724-33-9

For everyone fighting the good fight—
the ones who refuse to sit quietly on the sidelines,
who rise up, speak out, and stand firm
for those who need it most.
For the brave souls who keep showing up,
who keep believing, even when the world forgets how.
And for that rare, beautiful truth
we so often overlook:
sometimes, all it takes is one person believing in you
to change everything.

This is for you.

FOREWORD

Dear Reader,

Thank you so much for picking up *Some Like It Secret*! If this is your first time reading one of my books—welcome! I'm thrilled to have you along for the ride. And if you've been with me for a while, you might be thinking: *This title sounds familiar.* You're not wrong.

The first draft of this story actually dates all the way back to 2014. It was originally released as Book 4 in the *Going Royal* series, written to shine a light on some of the side characters we met in earlier books. I've always loved when a romance series takes a character you *thought* was in the background—and gives them the spotlight. That's exactly what I've tried to do here.

One of my favorite things about writing romance is that with every new story, I fall a little in love all over again—with the characters, with the journey, with the chaos and charm of their relationships. Whether it's the fake relationship of *Some Like It Royal*, the second chance romance in *Some Like It Scandalous*, or the delicious tension of *Some Like It Deadly*, each one has gifted me a favorite scene or moment I keep coming back to. And yes, *Some Like It Secret* is no exception.

A little peek behind the curtain: while I was writing this book, I had two beta readers reading along, chapter by chapter. One was firmly Team Sebastian and couldn't stand Meredith. The other? Hardcore Team Meredith, and completely blamed Sebastian. They read the *same exact scenes* —and had totally opposite reactions. I loved every second of it. But the real magic? By the end, they both agreed: it worked. And I was over the moon.

So, let me ask you something—have you ever wondered what would happen if a romance started *at the end*? After the break-up? No?

Well... I have a secret for you.

That's exactly where this story begins.

Like the other books in the series, there's plenty of rom-com charm here—but there's also a twist of suspense and danger that my newer readers will recognize as one of my favorite ingredients. I know I always say I'm excited to share a new story with you... but this one? This one feels extra special.

I can't wait for you to meet (or reunite with) Sebastian and Meredith.

Happy reading!

xoxo,

Heather

P.S. Wondering which scene is *my* favorite? Let's just say... it involves chocolate.

CHAPTER 1

SEBASTIAN

The click of the phone disconnecting echoed in his ear. Such a quiet, decisive sound should not be the punctuation mark ending five years together. Prince Sebastian Dagmar, Grand Duke, and second in line to a non-existent throne lowered the cell phone in his hand and checked the screen.

The call was indeed as finished as their relationship—or so she'd declared—because of some ridiculous blog report. He barely recognized the woman named in the report and—of all the false engagement stories over the years—why *this* one?

A flash bulb went off to his right. Another to his left. Sound rushed back in as a reporter yelled out a question and then another. Their interest in him waned swiftly at the arrival of the second car.

"Sir, we should move inside." Vidal leaned in and said the words in a soft undertone no one else would hear. Sebastian nodded once and re-

1

sumed walking, while he squeezed the phone in his fist. He'd walked red carpets so regularly beneath singular scrutiny so often, he was able to manufacture a smile and a nod as easily as he drew oxygen in and out. Both seemed rather impossible under the circumstances, yet he managed.

At the top of the stairs, Sebastian spared a glance toward his elder brother's arrival. Armand and his new wife made the perfect picture. The crowd gathered outside of...wherever the hell they were greeted them with loud cheers and applause.

"Vidal?" He glanced at his bodyguard. His nearly constant companion since before the death of Sebastian's father, Vidal had earned his trust over and over.

"Sir?"

"Where are we again?" Inside the event center, his detail closed around him in a phalanx.

"Los Angeles, sir."

"Good to know." The City of Angels—an appropriate graveyard to host the tomb of his relationship with Meredith. Vidal nodded and retreated a step. Sebastian drifted forward, soon immersed in the shaking of hands and innocuous small talk which accompanied attending such a social function.

Instead of relinquishing the private phone to Vidal's keeping, however, he slid it into his pocket in the vain, if somewhat desperate, hope that Meredith might cool long enough to call him back. The next three hours passed in a blur of speeches, toasts, and the requisite unimportant chatter over expensive plates of poorly presented chicken.

When the dancing began, Sebastian made a point to partner with all three of the unattached women he'd shared a dining table with—all perfectly pleasant and perfunctory. The moment he'd completed his duty, he detoured toward the bar and ordered a drink.

"Not the best idea." The quiet reprimand from Richard Prentiss, Armand's best friend and legal counsel, was an unwelcome intrusion to Sebastian's dour evening.

"Neither is it the worst." Sebastian nodded to the bartender before draining the glass in one long swallow. The burn of the alcohol did little to alleviate the frozen tundra in his soul. His control may not have been a match for his elder brother's, but Sebastian knew exactly what was expected of him. If he were to get utterly trashed over the next hour and make a spectacle of himself, most would only sigh and shake their heads.

What else did a second son do? His life, of course, was abysmally simple and utterly without complication or challenge. Fisting the thought, he motioned to the bartender. Richard leaned against the bar next to Sebastian, apparently not intending to leave him to drinking alone. Between his presence and the bodyguards, Sebastian enjoyed one of the quietest few moments of the evening—a perfect time to check his phone for new messages.

Richard's continued attention, however, interfered with the idea. After the bartender delivered his refill, Sebastian finally turned to study the attorney. "I'm surprised your fiancée isn't with you."

"No, you're not." The attorney's fast smile was easy and sincere. "She's working tonight and this is not her favorite activity."

Sebastian nodded. Kate Braddock worked personal security. Since her engagement to Richard, she only took certain types of clients—women in particular at a shelter Prentiss favored. She also avoided the limelight and, with the number of press present for the charitable function, she would definitely be in the spotlight.

"Well, please extend my regards to Ms. Braddock." He'd grown rather fond of the woman during Richard and Kate's sojourn on the yacht earlier in the year. She'd been recovering from wounds sustained protecting Richard and, while their presence required canceling his own plans, Sebastian couldn't begrudge either for the needed downtime on the open seas.

"I will be happy—" He broke off as Giles Corbin, a hedge fund manager, paused three steps away from them, his attention flicking between Richard and Sebastian. Richard's joining him at the bar was not happenstance.

While he was only the second son, protocol did prevent the majority from simply butting into a conversation. They waited to be acknowledged —well, at least those who wanted to be included in future conversations did. Clearly, Corbin wanted to speak to either Richard or himself.

Sebastian turned and motioned to the bartender. The second drink succeeded far more than the first. A third was definitely in order. "Do you want to talk to Corbin?"

"Not particularly, but it's better if he pitches to me." And by that, Richard meant it was better for the hedge fund manager to interrupt his evening rather than Armand and Anna's.

"You two look like you need to be rescued." Humor wreathed the familiar feminine voice and Sebastian turned to greet his cousin. Alyxandretta Dagmar Voldakov rarely stood on protocol and Sebastian's grin was the first unforced one of the evening.

"Your Highness." Richard inclined his head.

"You know better." She gave him a scowl, but Richard merely chuckled and excused himself. He headed out of the circle of security, one made slightly wider by Alyx's approach.

Catching Alyx's hand in his, Sebastian gave her a polite bow and then kissed her cheek. She accepted the affection graciously, squeezing his fingers once before moving to take Richard's place against the bar. Despite having taken the time to get to know her 'new' family over the last eighteen months, Alyx did not embrace public affection easily—save from her husband, Daniel.

Speaking of whom... It was unusual for him to be far from his bride. If anything, Sebastian admired how attentive the man was with Alyx.

"Don't worry. Daniel is talking business and I saw you over here looking forlorn, so I thought I would come keep you company." Alyx's quiet voice wouldn't carry and, even it did, no one was close enough to interrupt them. Not even the bartender, whom she waved off after he'd refilled Sebastian's drink.

"Are you sure you don't want some wine?" He considered slamming back the third drink as quickly as he had the first two, but restrained the impulse considering the concern on his cousin's face. Alyx was a couple of years younger than him and occasionally even more guarded than him or his siblings.

"No, thank you." She paused when the music changed and glanced at the dance floor. "I love this song."

Sebastian could not ignore the hint of longing in her voice, no matter how dark his mood. Pushing his drink away, he withdrew a step and extended his hand. Perhaps he couldn't make things right with Meredith immediately, but he could brighten Alyx's evening. "Would you do me the honor of this dance?"

A hint of a blush turned her cheeks pink, but her smile filled with delight. "Are you sure? What about...?" She mimed a small twirl of her finger to include their circle of security.

"We let them do their jobs," he told her gently, escorting her out to the floor. As expected, the men and women on duty widened their circle automatically, but Sebastian also knew better than to draw Alyx to the center, choosing instead an emptier part of the floor.

"I'm still not terribly used to having them shadow my steps—and before you start," she wrinkled her nose, exasperation lighting up the words. "I know *why* I have to have them. Daniel and Armand are thick as thieves on the subject."

He didn't smile, though her eyes twinkled with the invitation for him to join in her laughter. "You will get used to it." Years of living under the harsh lens of observation hadn't dulled him to its effects—or costs.

"I accept the concept, if only because I think I've finally gotten used to the idea people *want* take my picture, even if I cannot truly fathom why they think I am so interesting."

"It's not you—" When her jaw fell, Sebastian felt another reluctant smile tugging at the corners of his mouth. He genuinely liked his cousin. She didn't play any of the familiar games. "Truthfully, you are charming and a delight—but their fascination is with the idea of you and the crown. Some believe if they can touch a part of your charmed life, the charm will rub off on them."

"That is the most ridiculous thing." She halted mid-step and he paused obediently. "I have hardly led a charmed life."

"Again..." His smile faded as he coaxed her into moving once more. "It's not about you. It's about the position. An unfortunate by-product of our DNA in a world populated by social media and interaction is the public desire for wish fulfillment on their terms." Meredith never longed for either. She'd respected his position, but guarded against their exposure. While he'd delighted in their privacy, he'd also taken great pains to keep her protected.

7

The first waltz segued into a second and, when Sebastian would have guided her off the floor, Alyx looked at him imploringly. "One more? Please?"

Consenting, he drew her back into his arms. "It would be my honor."

Three steps into their second dance, all of Alyx's playfulness fled and he felt the full weight of her regard. The corner of his mouth turned up. He should have seen the ambush coming, but his lovely cousin was far more cunning than either of his brothers.

"Why are you so very sad, Sebastian?"

Though her question beckoned an answer, he could not indulge her curiosity. "It could quite possibly be the chicken. You did notice it was green, didn't you?"

The glib non-answer didn't satisfy his cousin. Her lips barely twitched. "You smile with your mouth and you say the words with just the right inflections, but your eyes are unhappy."

Far too practiced to allow her keen observation to rattle him, Sebastian smiled and let his affection for her show. "You have no need to be concerned, but your worry is sweet and I thank you for it."

"All right, if that's how you want to play it." Her candor never failed to entertain him. "But we are *family* and I would like to be your friend."

Whether it was the frustration underscoring her words or his own bleakness over Meredith, Sebastian couldn't say, but he wanted to put Alyx's mind at ease. Directing her to the edge of the dance floor, he halted and took her hands in his. "I would very much like to believe we are already friends."

His response elicited the most unexpected result. Tears filled Alyx's eyes and he went still. Awareness of their surroundings and the level of observation had Sebastian turning her away from the tables and clear of the other dancers.

With care, he slid his hand into the inside pocket of his tuxedo jacket and pulled out a clean, pressed handkerchief. Alyx accepted the cloth with a watery laugh and carefully dabbed at her eyes. "Victor would be horrified if my mascara started running."

"You look beautiful," Sebastian assured her.

Thankfully, her husband chose the moment to intercept them. With a cordial, if quick, nod at Sebastian, Daniel Voldakov slipped an arm around his wife. He kissed her temple gently. "Are you all right?"

"I'm fine, but Sebastian was very sweet and I think I horrified us both by bursting into tears." Another damp laugh and her smile grew in brilliance. "I didn't expect to be so hormonal."

Not quite wincing at the word, Sebastian made a point of looking elsewhere. This seemed a very private discussion to have in such a public place. Then her words registered, and he took a really good look at his cousin.

Alyx flushed under his gaze and, after a quick peek at Daniel, she gave Sebastian a secretive smile. "We're not confirming or denying anything yet."

Message received. "Please, let me know when I may respond to any confirmations or denials."

"I will," she promised and leaned her head on her husband's shoulder. "Do you think it would be poor protocol to slip away now?"

"Absolutely not. The dinner is done, as are all the tedious speeches. You have danced and smiled and been perfectly gracious." Catching her hand again, Sebastian bowed once more and pressed a kiss to her knuckles.

"He's right," Daniel agreed and nuzzled her forehead. "I've already asked for the car to be brought around. It was good to see you, Sebastian."

"And you, Daniel." Family did not have to stand on ceremony.

"Are you staying in Los Angeles for longer than a day this time?" Alyx asked. "We would love to have you over—dinner one evening, perhaps?"

Sebastian hesitated. He'd intended to leave the next day, but he hadn't alerted anyone to his plans, save for his security detail and pilot. "I am not terribly certain of my schedule." Not a lie. "I actually asked Vidal earlier what city I was in." Also, not a lie. "But I will call, and we'll make arrangements."

"Perfect." Alyx surprised him for a third time when she brushed his cheek with a kiss and paused to whisper, "I meant what I said earlier. I want to be your friend. I've seen the look in your eyes before on other people. If I can help—at all —please, let me." She squeezed his forearm once then allowed Daniel and their security team to escort her away.

He watched their exit silently and ran through his options. Switching gears, he glanced at Vidal. "I'm ready to go. Can you have security bring the car?"

"Of course, Your Highness. Destination?"

"The tower." For the time being, he'd return to his suite at the Petersburg Tower. It would have been readied for him, since his appearance at the event was on his schedule. "One last circuit and we leave."

"Absolutely, sir." Vidal and the others fell into step as Sebastian glad-handed his way around the room. A prince had a duty to be seen. He must be remembered as engaged and available, at least while on public display. He'd perfected the part. It took nearly an hour, but he finally made it out and pulled his tie free as soon as the car doors closed.

Leaning his head back against the seat, he retrieved his cell phone from his pocket. The screen was dark, though when he unlocked it, no messages waited for him. It was after eleven in California, which meant after two in the morning on the East Coast. She taught an early class and the last thing she needed was to be woken in the middle of the night, but he wanted to hear her voice.

If he took an early flight, he could be there by afternoon—or he could head to the airport immediately and be outside her class when she finished teaching. The car shifted abruptly and Sebastian glanced up at his driver.

"Apologies, sir. We have a couple of tagalongs." The driver explained and Sebastian sighed.

The press.

He couldn't go to the airport. Saying nothing, he slid the phone back into his pocket. Tomorrow he would call Meredith and make everything right again.

She was upset by their lack of time together. He understood her position and owed her an apology, but it would be better to let her calm before he confronted her. Anger sparked her declaration that they were through. His chest tightened. With her rejection, she'd thrown a gauntlet down, one he would gladly pick up.

They were not over. He'd protected her—cherished her—for too long to accept any other outcome.

But still, the ache in his heart wasn't assuaged. She'd never hung up on him before.

Never.

~

MEREDITH

Unsurprisingly, by nine-fifteen, Meredith Blake's eight a.m. class on the elementary theory of numbers struggled to focus on the whiteboard where she'd scrawled several equations. Other professors made do with only punching in their time in these basic courses, but Meredith liked to challenge her students. If any of them could solve the equation by the end of the lecture period, she gave an automatic grade bump to the assignment of their choice.

Application, after all, was the goal of number theory. Pacing to the front of her lectern, she studied the glassy eyed students arrayed around the room. Normally, she'd go for a joke or a light-hearted story, but she felt like she was dragging worse than they were.

Gravity remained unaltered by physical events, yet depression and disappointment seemingly increased her mass. How else to explain the weight bearing down upon her? Maybe everyone deserved a bit of a break. "Let's put it this way." She spoke in a clear tone and knew her voice carried all the way to the back row. With seventy plus students in these classes, projection was everything.

"Numbers are the basic building blocks of every single thing we do. We use numbers to predict the weather, to predict crime, to predict investments—even to predict winners. If you understand numbers and their applications, you have the most essential tools to success." Pausing, she let them absorb the information. Then pointed to the equation on the board. "Has anyone solved this?"

Not a single hand rose. She forced a concilia-tory smile, but instead of letting them off the hook, she said, "How many of you *tried* to solve it?"

Only two hands raised.

Well, two out of seventy-three weren't the worst statistics. "How many of you would have tried if I told you this formula will very accurately predict your chances of winning the lottery?"

Alertness sparked in her audience. Throw down a gauntlet, most people picked it up. Throw down the promise of money and those numbers increased. "I'll give you to the end of the week to solve the equation and send me your answer." But because she couldn't resist trying to make them smile, she said, "Of course, if you win the lottery with it—I'm sure my free grade bump won't be nearly as valuable, no matter how fun."

Laughter erupted and she nodded, satisfied. "See you all next week." Thumps of books, digital tablet covers snapping closed and the thud of feet on the stairs accompanied the students as they took advantage of their early release to rush out. All save Wes Keating and Rebecca Walsh—they headed straight for her. Holding up a hand, she stopped their questions before they could start.

"No, I didn't offer any other assignments for extra credit. No, I won't extend the deadline next week if you haven't solved it. And unless blood and bone are showing, you better have your assignments turned in." She raised her brows at their crestfallen expressions. "Any other questions?"

"No," Wes resettled his backpack "Thank you."

Rebecca sighed. "I was kind of hoping... maybe we could talk you into a second formula? You know, if we can't figure out the first."

Folding her arms, Meredith eyed the students. Every class always possessed at least one student who thought she'd change the rules just for them. "Sure, I can totally give you a second problem, however, you'd have to solve both for it to count."

The color drained from Rebecca's face. "I think we can stick to the first one." Tugging on Wes' arm, she led him from the lecture hall.

"That's what I thought. Have a nice day." She turned away because even what brief amount of amusement she gained from the interlude proved fleeting and she blinked back a fresh wave of tears. Gathering her notes together, Meredith glanced at the schedule on her phone. She held office hours in the afternoon and her schedule included two meetings with doctoral candidates to go over their theses.

Retrieving her purse, she felt the vibration of a second phone and sighed. She'd meant to leave it home when she came in for the early class, but some habits were impossible to break.

But I need to break them. Carrying the private phone, to which only Sebastian knew the number, was one such habit. Her heart twisted and her lungs felt like they'd seized. The hiccup in time couldn't have lasted more than a bare few seconds and yet she wanted to curl into a ball and cry all over again.

Her fingers itched to unzip the inner pocket

and pull the phone out. Any other day, she would have rushed to do so and asked him to hold on while she jogged across campus to her office. Once inside, she'd have locked the door, settled down behind her desk and—*Stop it*.

Just stop. Slinging the purse over her shoulder and stuffing the last of her things into her backpack, she refused to answer the phone. It wasn't any other day. Last night, after blogs broke the news of his 'secret' engagement, all the while another news channel featured his arrival at a posh event in Los Angeles, Meredith found she couldn't do it anymore.

Five years of passionate interludes when he could steal away from his life, of being at his beck and call and never knowing when his security would show up to smuggle her away, it was too much.

Under her arm, the phone kept vibrating. It would pause for a few seconds and then resume. A brisk wind cut through her thin sweater and she cursed herself for forgetting a jacket. This late into autumn, winter was a promise delivered at sundown. Though today it felt colder than when she'd walked to her class. She was frozen by the time she reached the building housing her office.

Bypassing the elevator, she jogged up the three flights of stairs in a vain attempt to alleviate her shivers. The news forecasted a cold front moving into the area later in the day, but Meredith suspected it already arrived. Exiting the stairwell on the third floor, she spotted Terry O'-

Connor leaning against the wall outside her office. The retired soldier straightened the moment he caught sight of her and a look, akin to relief, rippled across his face.

"I missed you at your class and you took a different route to the office today." Meeting her halfway down the hall, he tugged the backpack from her nerveless fingers and held out his hand for her keys.

"I didn't realize." Not really. She varied her routes depending on which lecture hall she needed to use, but they were all predetermined so Terry could track her as needed. Trailing him to her office door, Meredith shivered with an unexpected dread. The last time he'd shown up unannounced was after someone plunged a knife into Sebastian... "Did something happen?"

She'd made herself turn off the television the night before. A clean break was better all the way around, but what if something happened afterward? The attempts on Sebastian's family continued to increase and worsened in recent months and, while he didn't share the specifics, she was perfectly capable of reading in between the lines of news stories to speculate at what they didn't say.

Terry unlocked her door and glanced inside her office before allowing her to enter. "Nothing's happened, though I was instructed to pick up your detail today."

Instructed? Meredith deposited her purse on the desk. The crowded room boasted a variety of texts, some stacked ten and twelve deep on the floor next to her desk along with multiple white boards covered in equations. To the untrained eye, it probably looked like a lot of gibberish—a fact Terry pointed out on more than one occasion. Of course, he'd been to her office so many times at this point, the boards didn't earn more than a brief glance. "By whom?"

Instead of answering, he secured her door and prowled around to the window overlooking the quad below. With two quick twists, he closed the blinds before turning to face her. "By our mutual friend. Did you misplace your cell phone?"

Relief swamped her. Their *mutual friend*. Sebastian sent Terry to check on her—most likely because she wasn't answering her phone. If he'd called Terry, Sebastian was all right, at least physically. On the heels of her relief came resentment and its cousin, anger.

"No, I didn't misplace my phone." After circling her desk, she sat down then pulled her laptop out of the backpack. "I'm sorry he bothered you, but I am not planning on traveling anywhere. You don't really need to be here."

"I don't mind hanging out. You're good company and, if we're not traveling, I can catch up on my reading." He settled in one of her empty office chairs. "But you should check your phone."

Booting up her laptop, Meredith mulled Terry's advice, but didn't respond to it. Oddly, his presence and the crinkling of the newspaper he flipped open offered the most peculiar kind of comfort. Bringing up the college webmail, she skimmed the contents of her inbox without reading it. After several minutes of pretending to work and trying to ignore the insistent vibration in her purse, she retrieved the phone.

Forty-one missed calls and a fresh round of vibration.

She sighed. Bastian wouldn't stop. "Terry, do you mind?"

"Not at all." Her bodyguard—despite the years of acquaintance, it still struck her as odd that she had or needed a bodyguard—rose and folded his paper. "I'm going to the coffee cart on the first floor. Do you want anything?"

"A cappuccino would be lovely." With about three fingers of butterscotch schnapps in it, but she wouldn't ask no matter how good it sounded.

"You got it. Lock the door behind me. Don't leave till I come back." It was a familiar routine, but she nodded obediently and trailed him to the door. The vibration ended and quickly resumed. After locking up, she answered the call.

She couldn't say anything.

"Meredith?" Pure masculine sweetness poured over honeyed rocks flavored his European accent. Her pulse raced and her hands began to shake. "Meredith? Are you there?"

Falling into old patterns helped no one, least of all her. *Be strong. Don't tumble down this familiar path, no matter how passionate his response.* The man never failed to melt her past reason. A band around her chest squeezed all the air out of her. "I'm here," she managed to push out past the lump in her throat, then swallowed with difficulty. "What part of 'we're over' are you not understanding?"

Silence and then a whoosh of breath from his end. "All of it." His words grew more clipped in rebuttal. "I am sending the plane for you. O'-Connor will escort you to the airport and travel—"

"No." She didn't dare let him finish, since his words already weakened her. Her pulse picked up at the mention of his plane and heat flooded through her body. She couldn't see him. Maybe it was the coward's way out. God knew he was a fantastic lover and when they were together— yes, he focused one hundred and ten percent of his attention on her. No woman could withstand the sheer force of his personality and devotion.

But when they were apart? They were always apart. The time they did have together shortened repeatedly while the time in between visits elongated...

"Darling, listen to me. I promise, we will talk all of it out. I *need* to see you." Music to her ears, but how many times had he said the same thing before? Yet how many nights had she gone to bed alone, thousands of miles separating them and no one, not even her family, knew about the most precious relationship in her world?

"I said no, Bastian." Gripping the phone tighter, she tried to calm her respiration. Anger, resentment, misery, and joy tangled together in her stomach. An icy cold sweat broke out on her skin.

"Meredith, I am *not* engaged. I understand

the false story distressed you, but this is no different than all the others the last few years. Baseless speculation on the part of the press, their attempt to feed—"

"Actually..." She interrupted him before he went down the road of belittling her upset. He wouldn't mean to—he *never* meant to—but he would because he appeared to know better. He lived in a different world, one she wasn't even allowed to visit. "It is quite different. This time I don't *want* to understand. I don't want to pretend it's all right you spend half your life gallivanting around the world, dancing, kissing, and in general allowing all those women to be with you..."

His voice sounded tight when he snapped, "*They* are not important." Impatience fractured his normally calm and playful reserve, a first in their exchanges.

"Can't you understand?" She almost felt sorry for him, because he didn't seem to see it. Maybe he couldn't—maybe his upbringing precluded understanding the role of 'mistress.' "*They* may not be important, but they have easy access to you. You're not ashamed to be seen in public with them, and you certainly didn't seem to be fending off their affections. I teach math for a living, Sebastian. Maybe I don't understand protocol and politics, but I understand one plus one. Please respect my wishes, and leave me alone."

She hung up because if she didn't, he might keep talking and her traitorous heart would have listened. As she swiped away the tears on her cheeks, the phone began to vibrate again. She depressed the power button and held it down until the phone silenced.

It was over.

The sooner they both accepted it, the better off they'd be.

CHAPTER 2
SEBASTIAN

Sebastian stared at the nearly dead phone in his hand until a single knock on the door interrupted. Slotting it onto a charger, he slid it into the drawer. "Enter."

His brother's secretary, opened the door and curtseyed politely. "Excuse me, Prince Sebastian, but His Highness requests you join him in his office."

"I will be along directly. Thank you, Gretchen." He turned his attention back to the window and the sprawl of the city below once she'd closed the door. Though he'd expected a summons from Armand, he needed his mask firmly in place before he spoke to his brother.

Another knock announced a new arrival. Discipline schooling his features, he turned. "Enter."

Eduard Vidal stepped in and closed the door behind him. "O'Connor has Miss Blake under observation, sir. I've booked him for the full week and instructed him to keep a twenty-four hour

23

detail for the foreseeable future. He has two men he trusts on rotation for when Miss Blake returns to her home."

So, she wouldn't be alone and someone would be looking out for her. The thought provided a small measure of comfort.

"However," Vidal was not finished. "O'-Connor stated that if Miss Blake refuses protection, beyond reasonable measure, he cannot legally force it on her."

"The man can't follow instructions?" The last thing Sebastian needed was for Meredith to break away from her protection.

Unmoved by his annoyance, Vidal shrugged. "Your Highness, without her permission, it becomes stalking. As of yet, Miss Blake has not asked O'Connor to vacate, but it is a possibility."

Fine. He would simply have to deal with it before the idea occurred to her. Meredith had never shown any sign of rebelling against his need to see her safe before. Of course, she'd never told him they were over nor refused his calls before either.

Infuriated, he fought to control his breathing and lock down his reaction. "Understood. Please inform O'Connor I would be grateful if he would maintain his position for as long as possible."

"Do you still want me to make arrangements to send the plane?" Vidal's tone was careful, but beneath it lurked doubt. Sebastian couldn't really blame him for the question.

"Have it on standby. I don't want it going

anywhere. Also, inform the staff on St. Christos to ready the house." What he and Meredith needed was time away from it all. Together. If she felt neglected and underappreciated, then it was on him to fix it. "Please make sure no one else is there." The family's private island was one of the few carefully kept secrets guarded against the press and other interlopers. He'd never taken Meredith there, unwilling to share her with anything in his public life, but the only people who lived at St. Christos were trusted members of the staff, making it an utterly private paradise.

Vidal nodded. "I'll see to it."

Wishing he could already be aboard his plane or, better still, be in Boston, Sebastian made his way to the end of the long, cream carpeted hallway to Armand's office. His eldest brother of late eschewed their New York, London, and Paris holdings, spending more and more time in Los Angeles. At first, he'd attempted to foster closer ties with their newly-discovered cousin. More recently, Sebastian suspected Armand's reluctance to continue his usual duties could be attributed to his focus on his new marriage.

Gretchen rose at his approach then opened the doors with only a knock to announce him. Nodding his thanks to her, he entered and closed the doors himself.

His brothers occupied the conversation pit created by two sofas and a pair of upholstered chairs set in a loose circle around a Louis XVI coffee table. Though Armand worked in the space, he also used it for meetings. The casual atmosphere promised by the layout, fabrics, and color usage set his guests at ease—likely intentional on the part of the room's designers. Sebastian, however, saw past the façade of comfortable elegance to the office's true purpose.

George rose at his arrival, but Sebastian gestured for his younger sibling to resume his seat. Sebastian executed a half bow to his eldest brother, as was custom.

Armand merely raised his brows. "You're late."

"My apologies. I was detained by an unavoidable matter." He took a seat to Armand's right, opposite George. It seemed odd to have both of his brothers in the same room without others to play buffer between them. Armand maintained a careful distance since Sebastian admitted to outing his relationship with Anna to the press. Sebastian's miscalculation created a security snafu and headache, but ultimately worked in the manner he'd intended.

Armand was with the woman he loved. Pouring himself a cup of coffee, Sebastian waited patiently for Armand to tackle whatever subject led to his summons.

"George will be leaving for New York with his detail in the next couple of weeks. He begins classes after the first of the year." Armand didn't look at George, but their younger brother grimaced, obviously not looking forward to curtailing his lifestyle to procure an education. "As I'm sure you can assume, this will mean changes for your appearance schedule, Sebastian. Gretchen will update your secretary."

Unacceptable. "I will be unavailable for any significant appearances in the next few weeks."

"I beg your pardon?"

Sebastian refused to squirm under the weight of Armand's stare. "I have other commitments. I have no problem with taking on more duties at a future date, but as for the immediate needs? We'll have to send a representative or cancel."

"Or I can just maintain my schedule until Sebastian's free." George asserted his preference into the silence. "I can always begin in the fall semester."

"No." Armand dismissed the idea immediately. "You already put it off to the spring. You're *going*." Turning to Sebastian, Armand frowned. "I looked at your schedule this morning. I found nothing major pending which cannot be rearranged to accommodate George's appearances."

"Aside from several events coming in the next few weeks, I also need to make some adjustments for a matter which came up this morning." Unfortunately, Armand could and would make whatever changes he deemed necessary with or without his approval. Sebastian's duty was to see his requests were carried out. Whether they possessed a country to rule or not, as the head of the family, it was Armand's call.

"I'll be damned." George's tone spoke of awe. "I think our cousin was right, Armand."

"So I see. Excuse us, George." The clipped dismissal didn't sit well with their younger brother, and Armand spared him an inflexible look. "You need to go over your schedule with Peterson and his men. Do *not* be difficult."

Rebellious or not, George obeyed. As soon as the door closed behind him, Armand frowned at Sebastian. "What matter came up this morning?"

"It doesn't concern you or pertain to our family obligations. What specific items on George's schedule have to be covered? A presence at the critical appointments should be sufficient, yes?" He didn't need more responsibilities. His free time had been curtailed severely after an assassin got too close to him with a knife—the attack, along with increased tensions caused by Belarian royalists, demanded limitations to his schedule.

He was making plans to be with Meredith and would damn well not cancel them. Not while she thought herself less important than his duties—the thought so patently ridiculous, it aggravated him all over again.

Armand's eyes narrowed. "Everything about my family concerns me."

"Speaking of family, how is Anna adjusting to life as a Grand Duchess?" Bringing up Armand's new wife worked like a charm. His expression relaxed for a fraction of a second before a frown erased his good mood. No, he clearly hadn't forgiven Sebastian for his call to the press.

"Brilliantly, but then I expected nothing less. She is a force to be reckoned with when she wants something." He touched a digital tablet in front of him. "Out of George's appearances, the one which concerns me most is in Minsk."

"Minsk?" It was Sebastian's turn to frown. Though the Andraste family maintained extensive interests around the globe, they rarely ventured personally or with their capital into Belaria. Political unrest and threats traced back to the nation— "Why would you let him schedule something there?"

"I didn't." The quiet snap of the words rebuked him for suggesting otherwise. "However, with the unrest and the royalist movement and George's previous involvement, it seemed the most politically expedient way to put certain rumors to bed while mollifying both sides of the argument."

"And a good way to get him shot." Sebastian couldn't believe Armand even entertained the idea. "George is not the right man—" He stopped. "You never intended to send him."

"No. He started the mess." Armand sighed. "But I cannot be the one to go."

"No, since you're the one they want to crown, it has to be me." He'd walked right into the decision. As the second son, he was also Armand's heir, though George meant Sebastian remained somewhat expendable. If Anna gave birth to Armand's child, the family line would be secure and Sebastian's importance would diminish.

Thank God.

"You're the reasonable compromise. You are

unmarried, personable, and your reputation for being *bon vivant* makes you far less suitable to rule. Fortunately, despite one or two questionable choices, you have better impulse control than George." Somehow, the words didn't sound remotely like a compliment.

Belaria would be a security nightmare. The press was already primed for the Andraste family to make some kind of move. Their laser focus transferred from Armand to Sebastian with Armand's marriage—particularly since Armand and Anna denied the press a feeding frenzy by pulling off a very private wedding ceremony.

"You will, of course, receive additional security. Peterson will work out the specifics with Vidal, but I expect you to take every necessary precaution. We will double your security here and I've authorized the expenses to triple the force on the ground there. It will be three days in —one for an arrival and state dinner, a second for visiting key sites and the third for charitable foundation work."

Armand continued and Sebastian barely heard him. Certainly, three days in Belaria, but it would take weeks of prepping. The additional security and focus meant he wouldn't get anywhere near Meredith.

"Armand, I can't commit to this." He interrupted his brother mid-sentence, and Armand frowned. "I mean it. I have another crucial matter ..."

"*This* is crucial. These people are persisting in

their attempts against our family. They haven't targeted Mother yet, but I wouldn't put it past them. If Anna is right, Alyx will be announcing her pregnancy soon, and when she does..."

Sebastian's right eye began to throb. "The speculation begins." Alyx was a member of the family, but both her position as their cousin and her marriage to Daniel Voldakov removed her from the immediacy of inheritance. Armand's marriage, and his close ties to Alyx, made the speculation unavoidable. "Everyone will want to know when a royal baby will be in the offing."

"Exactly." Armand's stern mask relaxed and he leaned forward. "I have to protect Anna. *We* have to make this situation go away before the possibility occurs to them. The Belarian separatists think they want a royal presence, but the current government and military definitely don't want us there. They believe it far more expedient to eliminate our family line. Sebastian, I need you to do this for us. I *need* you to help me protect our family."

He could hardly say no, but Meredith needed him, too. How could he merge the tasks? He couldn't afford to ignore her repudiation. Meredith was a reasonable woman, but as long as several thousand miles separated them, he couldn't ensure she understood how much he cared for her. "I understand, brother, however, I need something as well."

"Name it."

It was a gamble, but perhaps after all these

years, Armand would understand. "Her name is Meredith Blake..."

~

MEREDITH

Freezing drizzle slicked the windows with the promise of ice by the time Terry pulled up in front of her brownstone. He'd insisted on driving her home, though she was less than a ten-minute walk from the campus. The proximity to the campus was one of the reasons she'd purchased the place when she'd accepted a tenure upon completion of her doctorate. "Thank you, Terry."

"You're welcome." He'd parked the vehicle and circled around to open her door before she'd gotten her seatbelt loosened. The man was almost preternaturally fast, but she'd gotten used to him over the years. Once, when she'd delayed meeting Sebastian because Terry hadn't been able to accompany her, Sebastian suggested replacing the man. She'd refused. Strange enough to have an escort in the first place, worse if the chaperone were a stranger. Terry was more than just a guard; he'd become her friend. Sadly, she and Sebastian's first real disagreement erupted over the issue.

Icy wind whipped around the side of the building and cut through her thoughts. She needed to stop dwelling on Sebastian and all the *could have beens*. Terry tugged her backpack from her fingers. He locked the truck up and walked her up the steps, one hand on her elbow. The steps weren't quite iced over, but if the weather forecaster was correct, dawn would be frigid.

"Do you have classes tomorrow?" Terry asked, waiting for her to unlock the front door. As soon as it opened, she crossed to the security panel and pressed in her code while Terry closed and locked the door.

"I have one lecture, but it's in the afternoon. I'll be grading papers all morning and I have to prepare for finals." With Thanksgiving just around the corner, the fall semester would tumble towards finals week before most of the students hustled off for the holidays.

"Can you do the grading from here?" Terry walked down the hall to the first floor sitting room then jogged up the stairs to the kitchen and her office. She trudged up behind him. He met her on the second floor. "All clear."

"Thank you, Terry." She didn't question him. The routine was too familiar. "Want some coffee?"

"Sure." He followed her into the kitchen. "What about tomorrow? Can you do your grading from home? If the ice storm turns vicious, it would be better if you did."

"You're worse than my father," she teased and went through the motions of setting up the coffee pot. She liked her brownstone and, while she didn't really need all the space, she enjoyed the kitchen most of all. It was huge and offered her plenty of room for cooking big meals or baking—she loved baking. Though it had been a long time since she'd hosted a dinner party of any kind, since Sebastian might call at any moment. Or, worse, the ever-present possibility she'd be paired with some poor man who thought they were on a date and then she would have to let them down easy.

Stop it. The constant mental chasing of her metaphorical tail would drive her mad. Maybe she could host a little get together over the weeks of Christmas break. Several of her colleagues wouldn't be traveling, so an evening with friends, perhaps some wine...

Stomach clenching, she pivoted on her heels. His back was to her, but maybe the answer she needed was right in front of her. "Terry? You're not married, right?"

His shoulders stiffened at the question, and he spun slowly to give her a guarded look. "No, why?"

"Would you like to stay for dinner? We've shared dinner before, but usually you eating in one corner while I work in the other. How about I make dinner then we sit down and talk?" She was babbling. She hated to babble.

The corners of his mouth turned downward. "I'm not sure it's the best idea, Meredith." She thought he would say more, but he went silent instead.

"Maybe not, but we're friends, right? Friends can have dinner." *Please don't make me sit in this house by myself. I don't want to cry myself to sleep, and I desperately need the distraction.* It would sound an awful lot like begging to voice the words, so she clenched her hands, digging nails into her palms. "If you have plans, ignore me. I've had a bad day."

He sighed, and shook his head slowly. "I don't have any plans, and I would love to have dinner with you."

"Fantastic." Shifting her attention back to the coffee pot, she glanced at her empty counters and grimaced. Figuring out what to have for dinner might be a problem...

"Want me to call and order something?"

She glanced over her shoulder. Terry eyed the empty counters with a skeptical look. "Actually, I know I have stuff here to fix. How do you feel about Italian?" Diverting to the pantry, she pulled out spaghetti and two jars of sauce. She'd hoarded it for a cold night like this one.

"Love it. I'll give you a hand..." He'd stripped off his suit jacket and begun rolling up his sleeves when his cell phone rang. Meredith nodded and went to get meat from the freezer. If she put it in water, it would defrost soon enough. Desperate for a distraction, she continued to pull out the pans she'd need and then went in search of the loaf of French bread she vaguely recalled buying a couple of days before.

Terry's voice was merely a murmur in the background until she heard, "Yes, sir. I'm with her now."

Meredith jerked around and banged her head against the door. The resounding crack actually made her see spots for a moment, and the half-formed headache of the day ballooned.

"Are you all right?" Terry lowered the phone and crossed to her as she rubbed her head.

"I'm fine."

"What's wrong?" Sebastian's voice echoed from the cell phone and Meredith's heart dropped.

"Let me see," Terry instructed before he ran his fingers over her scalp. She winced as he found the tender spot. "Go sit down, I'll get some ice."

"O'Connor." Clipped demand rang in Sebastian's tone, but it was a lower, more urgent note underneath it that compelled her.

"Don't yell at him, Sebastian. I banged my head. Give him a moment."

Terry pointed her toward a chair then he went to her freezer and pulled out ice. After filling a bag, he carried it over and pressed it to the side of her head before putting his phone back to his ear. "Miss Blake is fine, sir. She struck her head on the door and we're icing it." He went silent for a long moment and glanced down at her. She read the question in his eyes and shook her head. No, she did not want to talk to Sebastian. How many ways could she say it? "No, sir. I'm afraid I can't."

After another long pause, she could hear Sebastian's accent grow more pronounced even if she couldn't make out the content of his statements. English was a second or maybe a third language for him, and he slipped when he was well and truly angry.

"I understand, sir. But in this instance, my first and only goal is to see to Miss Blake's safety. I cannot and will not force her." Meredith blinked at the steel lacing Terry's words. "You are certainly welcome to do so, sir. I can provide you with several excellent recommendations."

No longer content to sit by while Bastian took his temper out on Terry, Meredith straightened. Her head pounded, but she didn't know how much was due to striking it on the door or Bastian's anger on the phone. "For what?"

"His Highness wants recommendations for personal security, Meredith. If you'll give me a few moments, I can help you with dinner." His expression softened, and his smile turned amused. For the barest moment, she glimpsed mischief in his normally serious eyes and Meredith's jaw dropped.

Terry was tweaking Sebastian quite squarely on the nose.

Oh dear God. She stood and set the ice down. "Terry..."

"It's quite all right. I have the numbers here, Your Highness." Amusement continued to widen his mouth, and Meredith scrubbed a palm against her face. Terry seemed to be enjoying the situation, but the plummeting sensation in her stomach worsened. Ending things with Sebastian shouldn't include hurting him. She wanted a clean break, not a painful one.

"I'll speak to him, Terry." The words slipped out before she could stop them and he paused.

"A moment, Your Highness." He depressed a button on the screen and she realized he'd muted the call. "You don't have to if you don't want to."

"He's firing you."

37

"He's entitled to do what he wants. It's not about you, it's about him asking me to perform tasks not outlined by my position. If you want to talk to him, I'll hand you the phone, but I don't want you to feel like you're being forced to speak to him."

Beyond the oddness of discussing her romantic contretemps with the man, it took it too far to put him in the midst of it. "I'm sorry," she murmured to him. "You shouldn't have to choose a side or be put in the middle."

"I don't mind," he told her with a level, serious look. "You tell me what you want and I'll make it happen."

She wanted to have never felt like she and Bastian couldn't work. She wanted for Bastian to have never been stabbed. Sometimes, she even wanted to have never met him. Unfortunately, time travel and magic were theories even mathematics couldn't turn into reality.

Yet.

"I'll talk to him." She held out her hand.

He passed the phone to her and then touched gentle fingers to the lump on the side of her head. It was still tender. "Put the ice back on this. I'm going to go down and move my car to give you your privacy. Do you still want to have dinner?"

She hesitated. Her impulsive request wasn't terrifically fair to him.

"It's just food, Meredith." He smiled, but the lightness in his tone did nothing to alleviate her guilt. "We can eat then I'll make sure you're secure before I head out."

Grasping his gracious offer, she found the wherewithal to smile. "Thank you, Terry."

"Of course, I'd do anything for you. Give him hell." With those bolstering words, he descended the steps and she unmuted the phone.

"Bastian, don't take your temper out on Terry..."

"I will do as I please with a man in my employ." *And wasn't that a high-handed statement?* "Why is he having dinner with you?"

"Can we not do this?" She pleaded with him.

"Meredith," his voice gentled immediately, and he sighed. "Are you all right?"

She could lie, but she didn't want to. Not anymore. "No, Bastian, I'm not all right. I haven't been for a long time, and I don't want to do *this* anymore."

"Darling, you're upset."

"Yes, I'm upset. I'm unhappy and I'm tired of feeling like the dirty little secret kept in the closet. I just want it all over. I want—" Everything. *You.* But she swallowed the words and fought the tears in her eyes. "I need to not do this. Can you please understand?"

"I *don't* understand." He gritted his teeth, and the grinding echoed over the line. "Everything was fine and then you tell me you wish to end it. No warning, no complaints—merely over. I *need* to see you. I know we can work this out if you will simply talk to me."

"Talking to you is the problem. We'll end up in bed and we'll make love and you'll say everything the right way, but at the end of it? I'll come back here, you'll go back to your life and *nothing* will have changed. I don't want to live my life on constant hold anymore. I can't do it. Everything wasn't fine and it hasn't been. Let me go. Leave Terry alone. Go find some princess you can crown or some other mistress to make you happy. I don't have it in me anymore." Tears slid down her face and she wanted to curse. She'd promised herself she wouldn't cry, but it hurt so damn much.

"Meredith, I don't want any other woman. I'll send the plane for you. Come, meet me. We'll talk. I promise not to make love to you until you've said everything you think I need to hear." Bless him for the irritated condescension in his voice because it worked to dry up her tears.

"I can't tell you how really generous of you the promise sounds." She sniffed and swiped away her tears. "But I told you no. I realize it must be difficult for you, Your Highness, to be told no. You'll forgive me for being crass, but I have tried to explain. You are refusing to understand. I will not be sent for. I will not be brought to you. The living for your beck and call part of my life is over."

"Don't. Hang. Up." The order rang over the line and locked her fingers before she could depress the end call button. "Meredith, you can be angry at me. You can throw things at me, but I will not *allow* you to ignore me. Do *you* understand?"

"Allow me?" Pulling the phone away, she stared at the empty screen as if trying to read his face thousands of miles away. If it were her phone, she might very well have thrown it across the room. Putting it back to her ear, she blew out a breath and said, "I'm not one of your—" The click on the other end told her he wasn't there anymore.

I'll be damned. He'd hung up on her.

CHAPTER 3
SEBASTIAN

After confessing his affair with Meredith to Armand, Sebastian excused himself to meet with Peterson and Vidal. Both men provided very clear visions of how they wanted the visit to Minsk to proceed. Sebastian listened and offered little in the way of changes, though he irritated Peterson by going with Vidal's specifics over his.

Unfortunately for Peterson, Vidal's personal efforts saved Sebastian's life. Twice. His actions lent weight and credence to his word over any other, even if the other person was the head of Armand's U.S. security forces. After the meeting, he walked into another with Anna and the Dagmar Foundation to go over a list of appearances they were hoping he could commit to, and a follow up meeting with the specifics of the foundation's goals in Belaria.

Six weeks was not a tremendous amount of time to plan a visit which would hopefully achieve Armand's agenda. The rushed nature of the planning sessions, coupled with their desire to limit the visibility of his public schedule all played an important role in the design. They didn't want to give anyone the idea of the visit's importance. He wished they could scrap the whole damn thing, but Armand was right. The family *needed* him to act.

By the time he returned to his suite, he was not in the best of moods. When his calls to Meredith's cell phone continued to go to voicemail, he ordered Vidal contact O'Connor. The call had gone less than well, though he'd been profoundly grateful to hear Meredith's voice.

The sadness in her tone cut deeper than the assassin's blade, which nearly killed him so many months before when it nicked his ribs and punctured his lung. Rubbing a hand against his side as if to soothe tentacles of remembered pain, Sebastian paced over to the window. He needed to go to Boston. If she required groveling to let him in the door, then he'd bloody well grovel.

But they needed to talk.

Why the hell is she having dinner with O'Connor? It made no sense. The man provided security. It was his job to oversee her general protection and to maintain a low profile, but he was there for her protection.

Furious and frustrated with the whole debacle, he was through with O'Connor stepping out of line. He'd all but sacked the man over the phone, and she'd rushed to his defense. Even her anger had been preferable to the tears shedding in her voice. He'd infuriated her on purpose, but it proved too easy. Regretting hanging up nearly as soon as he'd done it, he reached for the desk phone to order the plane.

The phone rang before he reached it. Unfortunately, he couldn't merely ignore it. He picked it up on the second ring. "Yes?"

"Come up to the penthouse." Armand didn't leave him any room to refuse because it wasn't an invitation. "We need to discuss your earlier matter."

"Of course." He didn't sigh or scowl. His brother expected his cooperation, so he would acquiesce. At least when he'd explained all of it to Armand earlier, his sibling actually listened to the whole sordid story without comment. If he'd summoned Sebastian, perhaps he'd come up with something to say on the matter. "I will be right there."

Disconnecting, he picked up his discarded jacket and checked his tie. Pausing for a moment, he adjusted the tiepin. A gift from Meredith their first Christmas, it was his favorite. Silver, it didn't quite fit with most of his ties, but his valet always managed to find one to match it. The penthouse was one floor above and the elevator opened as soon as he stepped out of his suite. Security released the elevator to ride to the top floor.

The family owned the Petersburg Tower and no one passed the thirtieth floor without clearance from security to access the family's private apartments. Kyle Johnson stood outside the penthouse door along with another man. Their presence warned Sebastian. Armand and Anna must be entertaining. Security did not maintain a presence on the floor when the couple was alone.

Not even if Anna began throwing things.

Johnson inclined his head and opened the door to admit him. However, not even the men at the door could have prepared him for the room full of people awaiting him. In addition to Armand and his bride, George lounged in one chair, while Alyx and her husband Daniel occupied one of the sofas. Richard took up another chair with his fiancée, Kate, perched on the arm. Stopping just inside the room, Sebastian frowned.

"Come, join us, Sebastian." Armand rose and walked over to the bar.

"Good evening." He paused to give Armand a bow. Straightening, he nodded to their family, but kept his gaze trained on his eldest brother.

Armand poured two tumblers and offered one to him. "I considered your tale from this afternoon at length. I've decided, in order to facilitate the best outcome, we should crowdsource your issue to the family."

Everything in Sebastian went still. He'd bared his soul to Armand in confidence. "I see."

"Do you?" His brother gave him a slow, almost lazy, smile. "I hope so. You were very helpful when I called you about Anna. One could even say too helpful. While your methods might have been questionable, your heart was in the right place."

"Armand." Anna rose and shook her head at her husband before coming over to give Sebastian a hug. After pulling back, she looped her arm through Sebastian's. "Ignore him. He was right to talk to all of us. We want you to be happy."

"Absolutely." Alyx leaned forward. "We want to help."

"I want to know how you kept it quiet for five years, brother." George eyed him with a bit more respect than he usually showed. Sebastian sighed —his discretion was something George might learn from, but he didn't know if he would advise taking such measures—except he'd had five wonderful years of Meredith to himself.

Richard grinned faintly when Sebastian's gaze alighted on him. "I'm just here to play billiards and have a drink."

"I'm with him." Kate jerked her thumb at her fiancé, her solemn expression unwavering.

"Remind me not to play poker with either of you." Sebastian tossed back his drink. No matter their reasons, they were all here. It was a show of solidarity and, while Armand definitely took the time to get his lumps in, his brother didn't tell him to deny her or end it. "Very well. I find myself in the unenviable position of having possibly made a muck of the best relationship in my life. What do you propose I do?"

His discomfort was a negligible matter if they could help him repair the situation. No one answered immediately. Alyx shifted and he zeroed in on the uncertainty in her expression. Catching his gaze, she winced. "I'm sorry. I want to ask a question, and I'm really not certain how appropriate it is."

"Ask." Sebastian couldn't possibly feel more

exposed than he already did. "Considering you were all invited to assist me in this matter, I will do my best to answer honestly."

"Why didn't anyone know you were seeing her?"

He shrugged. "Because I didn't want anyone to know."

"Not even your family?" The disbelief sliding under her words carried more than a hint of a rebuke.

Sebastian didn't look away. "Particularly not my family. I will not list specifics, however I have my reasons. While I will endeavor to answer relevant questions, I request in return you respect my privacy on all else."

"The moment the press gets wind of her..." Anna spread her hands expansively, alluding to the range of possible outcomes and the subsequent media feeding frenzy.

She would know. She'd not enjoyed a moment's peace once the press learned of her existence and her relationship with Armand.

"Precisely what I wished to avoid for her." Sebastian nodded to his sister-in-law. "Not to mention the security concerns."

"So what's the goal?" The directness of Kate's question carried no hint of judgment. "You were in a relationship with her. She broke up with you. Do you want her back? Do you want it all to go back to the way it was? What?"

"I want to *talk* to her." It sounded painfully simple, and yet...

"Which is difficult if she will not take your

calls." Armand caught Anna's hand and tugged her along with him. Seating himself, he pulled her into his lap. The very familiar and intimate ease said a great deal about their relationship as well as revealing the comfort they felt in the presence of their family.

"He could simply go talk to her," Anna argued.

Armand smiled and brushed a kiss onto the tip of her nose. "He and a dozen or so of the diligent paparazzi? I am certain the display would be quite romantic."

"Oh." She grimaced. "They really are annoying."

"Yes," Alyx agreed fervently. "Twice this week, two have followed me into the restrooms at separate events."

The mirth in Armand's face vanished and Daniel frowned, but it was her husband who spoke. "We'll talk with security. It won't happen again." The self-made billionaire made the statement with blunt authority. He shared a brief look with Armand, who nodded. They would handle it.

"Why don't you make a grand gesture?" George tossed out. "Take it public. It worked when you outted Anna."

"No." Armand echoed Sebastian's verbal refusal then continued, "We cannot control the variable of the press."

Returning to Kate's original question, Sebastian blew out a breath. "I want to talk to her. I've offered to send the plane and bring her somewhere private where she and I could talk. I think St. Christos would be the best location. It's private, isolated, and..."

"In another country. Nice brother, I never saw you as the type who'd kidnap his bride." George seemed to be taking far too much amusement in the situation. Silence reigned for a few minutes, but a movement drew Sebastian's gaze back to Alyx.

"You know if it's merely a matter of getting her somewhere to talk to her, you could do what Daniel did." His lack of understanding must have shown because Alyx's smile turned sheepish. "When he approached me about working with him, I'd initially told him no, rather pointedly, and I used a taser to back me up."

Anna and Kate both laughed, but Sebastian simply focused on his cousin and waited.

"Anyway, not to be deterred, Daniel posted an advertisement for an audition and the description fit me to a T. As it turned out, I was the only one who received the 'call' to audition..." She spread her hands and gave an artless shrug.

"I think it was quite clever of me." Her husband grinned.

"Don't be so proud of yourself. Although it was clever, you really annoyed me." She patted his leg, but her bemused affection gave her away.

Utterly unrepentant, the man laughed. "But the plan proved effective since you showed up without your taser."

"Armand made me come see him, too." Anna

interjected into the conversation. "A command performance because of the scholarship fund."

"I have apologized for my high-handed manner on many occasions." The stiffness in his brother's voice suggested he expected to apologize for it again.

"You have," Anna soothed him with a pat to his arm. For the first time since the 'consultation' began, Sebastian bit back a grin. "But my point is, Alyx is right. Sebastian wants to see her, so he may have to find a way to get her where he *can* see her."

Their point did possess merit. However, Meredith's refusal to speak to him put a wrinkle in it. She would simply turn down any business offers he presented via the family. She knew about Daniel, so using Spherecast as cover wasn't an option. He'd told her about his family, including the story of how Alyx reunited with them. She knew all the major players except...

Pivoting, Sebastian studied Kate with renewed interest. Kate did not attend the higher visibility functions. Although retired from her position as one of the family's bodyguards, Kate still did some work for Richard. She'd so far insisted the lower her profile, the better for their clients.

Kate met his scrutiny with a bland expression. "What?"

"She doesn't know *you*." A plan began to formulate as he turned the idea over in his mind. "You could go see her, get her to the plane and bring her to St. Christos." The room went silent as if everyone considered his words.

"I'm sorry." Kate blinked once. "You want me to go to—"

"Boston."

"Right. You want me to go to Boston, put her on a plane then shanghai her into leaving the country because she doesn't know me?"

"More or less. I know you're talented and she wouldn't be suspicious of you. Once she's there, I know I can smooth this over. It's a viable plan." For the first time since Meredith pronounced her desire to end things, excitement thrummed in his veins.

"Actually, it's a felony." Richard put a hand on Kate's leg. "Taking her out of the country compounds the issue."

"Not if she chooses to go." Of all people, it was Armand who answered. He wasn't looking at Sebastian, but at Richard. "He needs her to be some place where they can truly talk. With the limited timetable, St. Christos is the best location. You said she is a professor?" He switched his attention to Sebastian.

"Yes, applied mathematics. She's brilliant." The description didn't do her justice. Pride fisted in his chest. Meredith possessed the keenest mind he'd ever seen, and her gift with numbers seemed virtually miraculous.

"Wait, Meredith Blake? The author of *Applied Game Models using a Nash Equilibrium*?" Enthusiasm surged in Daniel's tone.

"Perhaps." Sebastian wasn't sure. He'd known she was published. In fact, he'd collected all her papers and repeatedly tried to read them. His lack of understanding didn't diminish his pride in her accomplishments. "She is truly gifted."

"She's an unqualified genius. You're going to need a better plan." Which didn't help him at all, but Daniel wasn't finished. "If she is who I think she is, invite her to a think tank situation. Suggest you want build new models using Return Times to create better advertising results."

"I'm sorry, he wants to ask her to do what?" Alyx twisted to stare at her husband as though he'd sprouted a second head.

"Return Times uses the structuring of probability to predict functions in social networking and media. It..." The software billionaire trailed off and studied the blank faces around him. "Does it matter what it does if it gets her there? It's an intriguing mathematical puzzle."

Meredith loves puzzles.

"So I take her an offer to do the number theory hokey pokey and, if she agrees, then what?" Kate considered out loud.

Richard nodded. "We tell her it is a proprietary project, research and development. Those are always quiet and require a nondisclosure. You can make the arrangements for her flight, but she has to board of her own free will *and* we have to accept she may turn the job down."

"Throw enough money at her and she'll say

yes," George offered to the rapidly formulating idea.

"She doesn't love money." Sebastian shook his head. "But she does love puzzles. We need to frame this as an impossible situation, the creation of a predictability model to help guarantee the drive of sales. So, instead of trying to predict a crowd, we'll frame the request as we want to build a model to help us predict one person. Her needs, her desires, and how to cater to them. If it works, we'll create the scenario in which she cannot say no because the outcome is what she wants as well." An outcome involving his presence in her life. He'd take her any way he could...

"Oh, I think it's the most romantic application of math I've ever heard." Anna's sigh pulled Sebastian from his thoughts. "Armand, we *have* to help him."

His brother chuckled and lifted Anna's hand to his lips, kissing her knuckles gently. "As you wish, my love."

"Daniel, can you write up the specifics of the different theories that might attract a professor of Dr. Blake's caliber?" Richard and Kate rose together, the two were so damn in sync. "Armand, we'll use one of the shell companies to host the offer. Kate, darling, do you mind flying to Boston? We'll arrange for a second, unmarked private plane to handle her transport."

With a few sentences, his family mobilized. Within minutes, they'd all gone off to tackle various tasks and Sebastian was left with his eldest brother.

"This may not work," Armand told him. "Are you prepared for the possibility?"

"As prepared as you were to lose Anna," Sebastian stated. She'd thrown him with her ending their relationship with no warning and her refusals to take his calls. "But once we are face to face, we can work out our differences."

"If she still doesn't want you despite such remarkable effort?"

He knew Armand wasn't deliberately provoking him, but the thought of losing Meredith for good was untenable. "Then I try again."

Whether it took five years or fifty, he wasn't giving up.

~

MEREDITH

Meredith stared out the window as the limousine pulled into a spot next to a private dock. The past several days elapsed in a heady blur and, after nearly a day of travel covering six thousand miles, she'd almost reached her destination. Of course, the presence of the speedboat suggested maybe she wasn't.

As soon as the car stopped, Terry exited then helped her out. Accepting his hand, she tried not to grimace as her muscles protested. "Still managing?" he asked.

"Just tired. " She didn't sleep on planes, not even luxuriously appointed private planes such as the one provided by Eridani Corp. After releasing his hand, she took a couple of steps and stretched. The warm breeze blowing in over the crystal blue waters was a far cry from the snowy temps of Boston. She'd stripped off the sweater she'd worn for the flight and stowed her coat with the luggage. Pushing up her sleeves, she glanced at their escort.

The enigmatic Kate Braddock served as her main point of contact since the request for her assistance on a proprietary study came in. Normally, so late in a semester, she would have turned it down flat. But when her department head approached her with the challenging proposition, it proved exactly what her beleaguered heart needed.

After contacting each of her doctoral candidates personally and making arrangements for her TA to handle her last three classes, Meredith believed she was more than ready to get away from her life, but nervous regrets plagued her on every step of the journey. She'd left behind the cell phone Bastian used to contact her and left the country without sending him any type of message.

How many times has he done the same to me over the years? I never knew where he was half the time. Only scant days since she'd broken things off, so part of her understood it was too ridiculously short a time to be *over* him, even if she was the one to end it, yet...

Terry touched her arm and drew her attention back to the pier. Their escort headed down to talk to the crew while a driver offloaded their meager belongings. She'd been rather proud of herself for packing only one suitcase for the trip, but it looked rather lonely with Terry's duffle bag. At least he'd packed even lighter than her. Ms. Braddock brought an even smaller bag.

"Are you sure you're okay?" It wasn't the first time he'd asked since they'd set out on the journey. His choice to accompany her on the trip surprised the hell out of her. It wasn't like before, when she'd flown off to meet Sebastian at some secluded location. Still, Terry merely shrugged. He still had a job—to protect her, and she wasn't going halfway around the world with a woman she'd just met whether it was for a special project or not.

"I'm fine," she assured him and summoned up a smile to hide the wilting sensation in her soul. Everything in her wanted to get back in the car, go back to the airport, fly back to Boston and get her cell phone. Stupid emotions. She'd never imagined herself as someone who would be a victim to her need for a man.

But Sebastian wasn't just any man—she loved him. Was *in love* with him. She wanted more than a few sporadic days and quick phone calls at random times of the day. God help her, she wanted a fairy tale, while the analytical side of her brain shook its head. What she needed was therapy.

"You don't seem fine." Terry waved off the driver and retrieved their bags. "If you want to change your mind, I can arrange transport for us back to the States. For the record? I think going home is exactly what you should be doing."

The offer surprised her, and she studied the stern line of his profile. Retired or not, Terry was a soldier through and through. Never completely still, his attention floated, always scanning the area around them. When he'd first come to work for Sebastian—and her, ultimately—his behavior used to unnerve her. So far from home, however, she found herself oddly comforted and irritated by it in the same moment.

In fact, Terry never left her side after the incident with Sebastian's phone call. His attitude, always protective in the past, seemed to be even more aggressive since she'd told him about the trip. Almost possessive. "Leaving aside the fact I signed a contract and a non-disclosure to do the work and I find their premise intriguing—what's bothering you?"

Kate returned before he could answer. "We're all set. It's about a two hour ride to the first island. We'll pick up a helicopter there..."

"A helicopter?" His voice deepened, and he took a step forward. The move was one he used to intimidate others, and she'd seen it work to great effect. Hell, it usually worked on her when she'd been in a bad mood over having someone 'escort' her.

Amazingly enough, Kate met Terry's gaze with aplomb Meredith envied. "You don't need to take the helicopter, Mr. O'Connor." Even the warm breeze seemed to chill under the blanket of ice in her voice. "You're only along because Miss Blake indicated she would be more comfortable with your presence. You don't have to go any further."

Tension ballooned in the air and Kate met Terry's fierce stare without flinching. When a thread of violence seemed to ratchet up into the intervening silence, Meredith touched Terry's arm. "Really, it's quite all right, Miss Braddock. I'm tired, and Terry's just worried about me." Walking between the two on purpose, she tried to send Terry the message to cool it with her eyes. Hopefully he understood because Kate fell into step with her.

"We can take a break here, if you're exhausted," the woman offered, her tone considerably warmer than when she spoke to Terry.

Meredith smiled—whether because of Kate's kindness or the gentle sway of the pier, she couldn't quite be sure. "Truthfully, I'd rather just get to our destination and hopefully have ten to twelve hours to pass out. I'm not a very good traveler."

"I noticed you didn't sleep on the plane." Kate paused as they arrived at the speedboat. The driver, a Greek man with swarthy skin and an easy smile, held a hand out to Meredith and she accepted his help to board. The tiny watercraft bobbed and he held onto her arm until she slid into one of the seats.

Kate boarded right behind her, sans any assistance, leaving Terry to board last. Taking the seat next to her, Kate adjusted her sunglasses and

Meredith fished her own out. The glare was a bit bright. Settling her purse into her lap, she glanced at their escort. The woman looked at ease wherever she was, no wonder she took care of the corporation's recruiting needs.

"I don't actually like flying." She was especially grateful for the boat, and a little more so due to Terry's strange animosity. It gave her something to focus on besides the helicopter ride. She'd only ever enjoyed a handful of plane rides in her life. Each time she'd been with... *Oh for the love of God, stop thinking about him.*

Kate shifted, and even with the sunglasses shading her eyes, Meredith could feel the weight of her stare. "You don't? Why didn't you say something?"

She laughed and it was the first real one she'd managed in days. It felt rusty even to her. "Because it's very difficult to ask anyone to wait two or three weeks while I book passage on cruise ships. It's a fear, and the only way to conquer fear is not to let it conquer you."

The roar of the engine firing up drowned out Kate's reply. Their pilot called something out and Kate responded. It was all Greek to Meredith. A fresh wave of humor bloomed inside of her, and she giggled. A glance at Terry earned her a tight-lipped smile and some of her newfound cheer diminished. He wasn't pleased.

The boat pulled away from the dock and they raced across the waves. Meredith forgot all about Terry's bad mood, her own discomfort at flying, and even her exhaustion. The wind pulled at her hair and she was grateful she'd pulled it all back into a ponytail. Scents of salt and water twined in the air around her, both bracing and refreshing.

If something could smell exotic, then she'd found it. Meredith leaned forward for most of the next couple of hours. She'd been on her fair share of ships, from skiffs to yachts, but the speedboat sliced across the top of the water like it rode the wind and she couldn't get over the wild freedom it promised.

Note to self, she'd decided by the time she saw the island in the distance. *I have to do this again.* Maybe she could take a trip the following summer, and pilot her own speedboat. *Wouldn't that be a kick in the pants?* Just wait until she told...

Meredith sighed and sank back against the seat, another layer of her good mood evaporating. Apparently, not thinking about Sebastian would take some practice.

Twenty minutes later, she stared at the helicopter where Terry stowed their gear with gut wrenching terror. It was so tiny. Well, compared to an airplane at least. The helicopter seemed designed to seat ten people, and only Kate and Terry were joining her in addition to the pilot.

"Three things to remember." Kate came to stand next to her, sunglasses still shielding her eyes.

"And they are?" Meredith couldn't get her racing heart to slow from a gallop. It felt like it wanted to beat right out of her chest and sweat slicked her spine. Thank God she hadn't eaten anything since London or she might have already thrown up.

"I'm a licensed pilot. I can handle this craft. It's rated in the top 99th percentile in safety and performance." Okay, the information sounded a little better. "Two, we're not flying especially high. We'll be within a couple of hundred feet of the water. Worst case scenario, you're going to get wet."

Twisting, Meredith stared at Kate. Was the woman serious? "Do I dare ask what the third thing is?"

The corner of Kate's mouth twitched. "There are no sharks in these waters."

A giggle slipped out before Meredith could stop it and her sides actually pinched as laughter shook her. The absurd dissemination of information burst the fear spiked tension locking up her muscles. "I like you," she volunteered.

Kate chuckled and nudged her toward the helicopter. "Ditto. Now let's get you strapped in."

Terry's sour mood seemed firmly in place, but he still helped Meredith into the copter and took the seat next to her. Terry buckled her in, not Kate. The other woman took the seat opposite them, her expression unreadable as she watched. The big door closed and the rotors started to spin outside. All at once, Meredith's stomach plummeted and her heart picked up the pace.

She was going to throw up.

"Miss Blake?" Kate called, leaning toward her. "I forgot to ask—"

"You forgot to ask what?"

"Can you swim?" The dry question lanced the fresh bubble of fear and Meredith started giggling again. When the laughter precluded her answer, Kate pulled off her sunglasses. "No, seriously, can you swim?"

Meredith laughed harder. It was all so silly, yet so fun. She was on an adventure. When she caught Terry staring at her with narrowed eyes, another fit of giggles erupted. Before she knew it, they were airborne.

Excitement coiled with anticipation, so she gripped the armrests until her knuckles turned white. Terry put a hand comfortingly over hers, and her laughter faded. Waiting a beat, she found a quick smile of thanks for him and then pulled her hands into her lap and looked out the window at the water as the island vanished.

From the corner of her eye she caught Kate looking at her. Terry's attention was elsewhere, but Kate shifted her gaze to him and then back to Meredith, a question in her expression. Yes, Meredith didn't care for Terry's behavior, but no —she could handle it.

She shook her head once and Kate nodded. If nothing else, this adventure introduced her to Kate—she was something else. Maybe they'd have time to get to know each other around the assignment.

"Fifteen minutes," a voice announced over the intercom. "And we've been cleared to land."

Oh. They were almost there. Amazingly enough, the minutes passed quickly and then they landed with a bump, which made her stomach summersault, but at least it was over. Kate exited ahead of her and Terry went next. Meredith was grateful for the reprieve because her legs trembled violently and she felt shaky all over.

It was probably exhaustion coupled with hunger. A shower, some food, and a good night's sleep and she would be ready to tackle the Return Times challenge. Some of her relish for the project resurfaced. Unfortunately, she couldn't avoid Terry's hand as he helped her down. She mouthed thanks and pulled her hand free, ducking even though the blades were much higher than her head—they were still spinning.

Slowing, she lifted her head to take in their surroundings. It was a lush paradise with deep green grass and trees on one side of a thin ribbon of a road and beautiful white sand beaches and azure water on the other. A car waited for them and Kate was on her way to it.

Following, Meredith tried to quell the tremors rocking through her. Then the backdoor of the car opened and he stepped out. She felt stripped to her soul. Ice cooled her skin even as heat burned in her blood. The oxygen seemed to get knocked out of her lungs as the most handsome man she'd ever known stood, waiting for her.

The wind tousled his black hair and a lock of it fell down on his forehead. She knew his eyes would be the shade of onyx, so dark she wouldn't know where the pupil ended and the iris began. He wore a white shirt, with no tie or jacket and white slacks. They highlighted the deep bronze of his skin, and he looked like a god come to life. Even the shadow of scruff darkening his jaw added to the raw sensuality of the man.

She couldn't breathe.

Bastian...

That son of a bitch.

CHAPTER 4

SEBASTIAN

Sebastian tried to keep his lust under control, but the tight leash he'd forced over his reactions since Meredith's fateful phone call slipped and need bucked all convention. A ray of sunlight framed her perfectly. Meredith never hid behind layers of couture, coifing and cosmetics like a plastic doll come to life. She'd always been more. Softness, heat, and utterly feminine—she'd kindled a wild possessiveness and desperate need to claim her from the first moment they'd met.

The familiar fire exploded to life and surged in his blood. Question filled her features and her mouth fell open for the length of a heartbeat before she snapped it shut. Fury replaced shock, but before he could respond to any of it, Kate stepped into his line of sight.

"You really should have waited at the house," the former bodyguard murmured. "I don't think she's ready to see you, and we need to talk—"

"No," Meredith's voice rang out from the tarmac, and she turned to get back in the helicopter.

Cutting around Kate, Sebastian strode toward her. He was not letting her leave, not before they talked. "Meredith—"

He didn't make it a half-dozen steps before O'Connor stepped into his path and body blocked him. "You need to back off."

A moment later, Vidal drove O'Connor back, inserting himself between the prince and the guard. Violence thrummed in the air and Sebastian's gaze hardened as he pinned a glare at the bodyguard tasked with Meredith's safety. The same man who'd been having dinner with her, whose touch lingered on Meredith's hand and arm longer than necessary.

"Stand down," Vidal ordered in a cold, cutting tone, but the command had little effect on O'Connor.

"You tell him to keep his distance. She doesn't want to see him and he doesn't get to use his position to force the issue." He shook off Vidal and shifted his weight. The two were squared off and Vidal didn't retreat a step. The rest of Sebastian's detail surged up around him. O'Connor's hand shifted and, for a fraction of an instant, Sebastian thought he might actually go for his gun.

Switching his attention to Meredith, Sebastian's heart stopped when she rushed forward and put a hand on O'Connor's arm. "Terry."

She was too damned close to him and the man adjusted his angle to put her behind him. *Too damn close.* "Meredith, come here." Sebastian issued the directive and—although he was fairly certain O'Connor wouldn't harm her—he refused to take any chances with her safety.

"You stay where you are." O'Connor countered with his own order. Tension crackled in the air.

Bracketed by two more of Sebastian's detail, Vidal invaded O'Connor's space. "I told you, stand down."

"Meredith, get away from him. *Right now*." Sebastian wanted her out of the rapidly escalating showdown. She hesitated, glancing from O'Connor to him and then pulled her hand from the man. When O'Connor intercepted her step away, the violence exploded.

Vidal struck O'Connor's arm while a second bodyguard hit him full in the chest. The third man scooped Meredith up and jerked her away from the fray. Sebastian retreated with her, wrapping his arms around her and pulling her toward the car. It was over in seconds, with O'Connor pinned.

Gasping with horror, Meredith strained at Sebastian's hold. "Terry, stop. It's all right. Please, Bastian, make them stop."

He'd rather dump the ass back on the helicopter and ship him off the island, but he couldn't dismiss the worried look pinching Meredith's features. "It's all right," he soothed, rubbing her arm. "Vidal."

The head of his security detail rose and they brought O'Connor up with them. Vidal removed his weapon and unloaded it before retreating a step to look at Sebastian. "Your Highness, you and your guest should go to the house. We'll settle this issue here."

"Settle it?" A tremor fractured Meredith's tone. "No, Terry goes with us. This is a misunderstanding. There is nothing to be settled."

Her immediate defense chafed and Sebastian clenched his teeth.

"You know what would help, Meredith?" Kate was suddenly on Meredith's other side, drawing her attention away from the scene. "You and Sebastian go chat. Let these men settle it as professionals. Everyone is a little one edge and they aren't going to calm down until all protectees are in a secure location."

Richard Prentiss' fiancée wasn't finished, she swept a cool glance over them. "In fact, I'll take over, along with Michel here." She indicated the bodyguard who'd stayed with Sebastian. "You four figure it out and, O'Connor, I'd like to remind you that I and the helicopter are still here. You can go back with me."

If Sebastian wasn't mistaken, Kate actually sounded like she relished the idea of O'Connor fighting her on the issue. Irritation turned to concern at Meredith's trembling beneath his arm.

Ignoring the others and focusing on her, Sebastian lowered his voice. "Come with me. It will be all right, I promise. No one will hurt him." No matter how he might wish it otherwise, this wasn't about her bodyguard, but her. Meredith was the only one who mattered.

"I can't believe you did this." Emotion quivered in her voice and she strained to pull away from him again. This time he let her go. When she took two shaky steps toward the car, he followed—ready to catch her.

"I needed to see you." He wouldn't apologize for it, but he would say, "I'm sorry for the scene. I did not expect O'Connor to object so strenuously to our speaking."

"What does that even mean?" She whirled to face him, halting halfway to the car. Kate and Michel still stood between them and the others.

"I missed you," he told her simply. "We need this time together. We need to work out whatever issue convinced you to try and end us."

Her cheeks went scarlet and she shot a glance past him to the others and then back. Lips clamping together, Meredith pivoted and strode toward the car with Sebastian keeping pace. He made it a step before she did, waved off Michel and opened the door for her. She slid inside and he followed.

Kate caught the door before he could close it. "We're going to take care of this. I'll follow in the second car." Her gaze went past him to Meredith briefly and then back to him. With a warning look, she closed the door and patted the roof. The driver pulled away immediately.

"Why did you do this?" So low was Meredith's whisper, he strained to catch it.

"Because you wouldn't talk to me." Leaning back, he tapped his fingers against his thigh. What he wanted to do was wrap an arm around her, but her stiff posture, the way she angled to look out the opposite window and her still folded arms all screamed 'keep away.'

"So you just decide to invade a meeting where I'm supposed to be—" She broke off and twisted, her wounded gaze striking him like a physical blow. "There's no job, is there?"

Turning sideways, he put his arm on the seat behind her. "No, I'm sorry. When you refused the calls and not even O'Connor could get you on the phone, I needed to take some drastic measures."

"Drastic? Really?" Her mouth opened as though she intended to say something else and then snapped shut again. When she gave him her back, her spine ramrod straight, he scowled.

The drive from the landing pad to the house was mercifully short. The moment the vehicle came to a halt, Meredith fumbled with the door and pushed it open, all but spilling out to walk away with jerky motions. Following her, Sebastian waved off the men coming to greet them.

"Go away," he ordered and strode after Meredith. Clearly an audience was impeding her ability to speak. When she didn't slow, he caught her arm. "Meredith, we're alone you can—"

"You son of a bitch. Who do you think you are?" She whirled, and her palm slapped his face with a sharp crack. Angry fire snapped in her eyes and her face flushed with temper. *Well, at least she isn't walking away.*

~

MEREDITH

The moment her hand connected with his face, regret and the horror set in. Meredith jerked back a step and covered her mouth. "Oh my god, I'm sorry."

"No." Sebastian wore a rueful expression and shook his head. The white mark on his face from where she'd struck him turned a livid shade of red. "I deserved it."

She was shaking from the inside out. Yelling at people. Hitting them. This wasn't her. The pattern of irrational, nonsensical behavior defied convention. "I can't believe I hit you."

"I always said you were the passionate one." The corner of his mouth curved upward with the familiar teasing words and her rebellious heart squeezed. Even the evidence of her slap couldn't diminish his charm.

"Oh God, Bastian. This is not how I pictured any of this." She pulled the band from her hair and freed her ponytail to ease some of the pressure on her skull as she stared at him. The riot of her emotions tossed her down the rapids to bang off rocks of frustration, longing, anger, and need.

All at once his face gentled and he closed the distance between them. "Nor me. I'm so glad you're here, so if you need to yell at me or hit me again to get it out of your system, then do it. But promise you'll talk to me afterward." Artless charm, and playfulness underscored the sober conviction in his expression. "Tell me what I did wrong, so I can fix it."

"You didn't do anything wrong." As painful as it was to admit it out loud, it was true. He'd never been anything but himself. "I—I just can't do it anymore." She'd rehearsed the words she'd used in their phone call for three days before she'd gathered up the courage to make it. Confrontation was not her forte. She could handle teaching a class or addressing a thousand-person-filled auditorium—as long as it was on numbers, formulas, or equations—but Bastian turned her inside out.

He studied her and eased forward another step. The fingers he touched to her chin were inexorably gentle. He nudged her gaze up until she met his. Shame and regret twined through her. "Talk to me, darling. Something triggered your call. Everything was fine and then..."

"Don't you see?" She took hold of his hand on her chin and he closed his fingers around her, tugging her closer. Surrounded by the meticulously tended grounds and balmy breeze, she felt about a thousand miles away from their problems and yet—the whole situation was such a perfect metaphor for all of it. "Everything wasn't —isn't fine."

His frown suggested he didn't like hearing the information, but he nodded once. "All right. What happened?"

There was the rub. "Nothing." After squeezing his hand once, she made herself let go of him and retreat. His nearness made it impossible to think clearly, not when all she wanted to do was to peel open his shirt and inspect every inch of his gorgeous body. Need settled like a hot coal in her belly and she bit the inside of her lip.

Pain served as a stinging reminder to not fall into his arms. God knew, sex had never been their issue. She tried to concentrate on their surroundings—an island in the middle of the Mediterranean. Her circuit brought her around to face the house and she stared up at the magnificent mansion. Constructed of almost rose-colored stone with soaring windows and at least three, if not four, levels—it was beautiful.

"I find 'nothing' difficult believe," he said carefully into the hollow silence. "One does not simply end five years of...anything for nothing." The hesitation raked bloody scores through her soul.

Their relationship lacked definition. He was a prince. She was a professor. It was almost a sitcom, yet she found nothing funny about it. "It's been months since we've been in the same place for longer than a day."

His brows drew together with his frown, but she didn't see anger—only intense thoughtfulness. "Yes, we were supposed to have a week on the yacht and I should have made the delay up to you sooner. I was not expecting Armand to send Kate and Richard there for Kate's recuperation..."

"Wait, Kate is the attorney's fiancée? The one who was shot?" All of a sudden, Meredith felt like a horrible person. She'd not known who she was, and Kate had been so kind to her while duping her into this visit.

"Yes, but as you can see she is fine. She

needed a few weeks to recuperate. Armand was far more comfortable sending them to the yacht to be secure while she did so." He reached out for her again, but she avoided his touch. With a sigh, he slid his hands into his pockets.

Meredith paced away again, fighting to keep tears at bay. "I'm glad she's all right. I understood why they needed a place to go..."

"I promise, I will make our lost week up. I know we got off to a poor start here, but we have the island to ourselves for the next couple of weeks. It will just be you and me—"

A throat clearing interrupted him, and Meredith glanced back to see impatience darken Sebastian's countenance. Vidal, Sebastian's head of security, stood a few feet away. "Please forgive the intrusion, Your Highness."

"Can't it wait?" Sebastian didn't take his gaze away from her and she wrapped her arms around herself. They were standing out in the open and they were hardly alone. Security moved to the fringes, save for Vidal, but she could see them arrayed out in a loose circle with several yards between them. Chances were they couldn't hear anything.

"My apologies, Your Highness. It cannot."

Aggravation slid over Sebastian's face and vanished so quickly, she thought she might have imagined it. "Please excuse me, Meredith. I will be right back." He pivoted and the pair walked several feet away. Beyond them, she saw cars in the circular drive—Kate walked down the front steps and spoke to Terry as he exited one of the vehicles.

Kate greeting him didn't bother Meredith nearly as much as the very obvious security presence around Terry. Two of Sebastian's guards bracketed him. He was in trouble because he'd interfered and tried to protect her.

Abandoning her position, she strode toward the cars. The men noticed her approach right away, but she ignored them all except for Terry. "Are you all right?"

"Nothing wounded beyond my pride." He gave her an easy smile. "How about you?"

She waved off his concern. "You're not in trouble are you?"

"You assault the boss, you get in trouble." His chagrined expression mired her in guilt.

"You were doing your job." She frowned and glanced over to where Sebastian and Vidal spoke. Sebastian's gaze was locked on her and the frown on his brow deepened. "I'll talk to him..."

Terry caught her hand and tugged her back before she could take a step. "You don't have to." He dropped his voice. "In fact, I think it would be better if you didn't."

Very aware of the eyes on them, Meredith lowered her voice. "You shouldn't be in trouble for protecting me."

"Don't worry about me. I mean it. Can you handle this?" He dropped his voice as well.

"I have no idea." It was the truth. She really didn't know how she was feeling at the moment.

"I'm sorry I got you into this mess. You told me I should reconsider the job offer when it came in."

In fact, Terry was the only one who counseled her to think the entire thing through. She longed for a distraction and her department head had been over the moon at the idea of the donation and projected grant money the work could generate—not to mention reputation. If she published again, it would have been five major accomplishments in five years. She was at the top of her field and the project would have sealed it.

She'd understood Terry's caution, but at the time, she'd wanted to leave more than worry about impossible scenarios. What she wouldn't give to be back in Boston, freezing in class and teaching algorithms.

"Meredith?" Sebastian's voice washed over her and guilt gnawed at her. Her earlier wishing that she hadn't met Sebastian was less than charitable and completely untrue. Squeezing Terry's hand in a show of solidarity, she released him to look at the love of her life. Her heart did another little flip-flop in her chest.

Yes, she was angry and she was frustrated, but, no, she didn't want to be in Boston. She didn't even want to be standing outside the house. She wanted to throw herself at Bastian and lose herself in his arms.

"All done?" Her attempt to go for a brighter tone sounded odd to her ears and, based on Sebastian's narrowed gaze, his as well.

"Quite." But for the first time since she arrived, she heard a note of question in his voice.

He held out his hand to her and even though she knew the rational choice, the smart choice, would be to close him out before he battered down her fracturing defenses, she slid her palm across his.

The touch sizzled and when he drew her close this time, she went. He said nothing to Terry or the others, but led her up the stairs. Threading their fingers together, she sighed. "Going to give me the ten cent tour?"

At the top of the steps, he paused. "Do you want one?"

Despite her exhaustion, and her teeter-tottering emotions, she did. It might give them something to talk about and ease the jagged chasm between them. "Would you mind? I—" She canted her head back and looked up at the huge house. "I've never been here before." It sounded so flimsy, but if Sebastian disagreed with her, he didn't let it show.

"I would love to show you the house." He slid her arm through his. The guarded look she'd glimpsed earlier seemed to retreat behind his playful countenance, but it didn't disappear entirely. "St. Christos has a history, but the house has only been here for about fifty years or so. My grandfather built it for my grandmother..."

He led her inside and his accent washed over her as he shared the story. The interior of the house was nearly as spectacular as the exterior and yet, as fine as it all was, it also possessed the curious effect of looking like a real home. Every room seemed designed for comfort and family photos scattered across the various tables.

She recognized what had to be his forefathers—or maybe even his father—in one of the paintings, since he looked exactly like Sebastian. Of course she knew what his brothers looked like and, while Sebastian and Armand favored each other, George looked more like their mother.

The closer she came to the painting, the more of Sebastian's likeness she saw in the older, distinguished gentleman. Grave eyes gazed out from the handsome face and a touch of silver highlighted the man's temples. While it was only an oil painting, somehow the artist seemed to have captured something of the man's personality—*or maybe I'm just reading something into it, but this could be Bastian in a few years.* Something deep inside her loosened, and her throat went scratchy.

Bastian would look the same, with serious eyes and the hint of weathering to his otherwise beautiful face. The silver crown would be a testament to his age, but would he be lonely? Who would walk through those years with him? Or would he...

"You're not listening to me anymore," Sebastian murmured from a step behind her and Meredith blinked back the tears desperately pooling in her eyes.

"You look like him," she said, and bit her lip at the choked sound she made with the words.

He turned her around and caught her face in his hands, swiping away her tears with his thumbs. "Darling, what? What's eating you up inside? Something's upset you deeply, and I can't fix it if I don't know what it is."

The desperate desire to avoid this very conversation drove her from the beginning. Five years of wonderful adventures and magnificent moments, but all of them fleeting. She lived in Boston, while he roamed the world. "Us. We're never going to work," she whispered, and hated herself for saying it. "I don't belong here and you? You have so many important things to do."

"*What* are you talking about?"

"I'm talking about you and me. You have events, and duties and responsibilities and—" She sniffed. God she hated losing it in front of him. She was a terrible crier. "I have students and projects. I shouldn't even be here now. The university is going to be disappointed and, well, it was a project which could have garnered them future grant money..." And she rambled, wincing at her scattering focus. She fought for a weak smile. "I'm tired. I'm sorry, I know I'm not making any sense. It's just, after this last year, what you and I have? It's not working anymore. You were stabbed, which changed everything..."

Why couldn't she explain it right?

"I'm sorry my injury inconvenienced you." His stiff tone carried a note of warning.

Stumbling over her own guilt, she stared at him. "Oh, don't say it like that. I was terrified for you, and it was weeks before I heard anything. Nothing in the press, no phone calls. Not even a cryptic note with a puzzle."

"Security was impossible for a time. My

brother monitored every incoming and outgoing communication." The corners of his eyes tightened and his mouth compressed into a thin line. "I will make arrangements to ensure you are never left to wonder again. I told you when I called you—as soon as I was able—why I hadn't been in touch. Security was very much an issue."

"That part, I got. Terry practically moved in with me for those few weeks—" Apparently it was the wrong thing to say, because Bastian's gaze slicked over like ice.

"He did *what?*"

A pulse-pounding headache began behind her eyes. "He told me there were issues, so for the time-being, he wanted to keep a closer tab on me. There was no sense in him staying in his car when I have three bedrooms." She so did not want to talk about Terry at the moment. "And, yes, you did tell me there were security issues, but those *issues* certainly didn't stop you from partying on the yacht during the same time-frame. I saw the special. During at least one of the weeks you were 'locked' down, you were entertaining any number of beautiful women."

"Appearances needed to be kept, and I was barely there. I spent most of the visit below decks recuperating while they occupied themselves. I should not need to defend the choices security makes. It was a very crucial time."

"Of course you don't, and why should you explain it to me? You've told me you were too locked down to make a call, but obviously having a number of nubile bodies dancing around was a precaution... Yet another reason why we don't work." As much as the loss wounded her, it did manage to dry her tears. She tried to back away, but Sebastian's arms came around her and dragged her against him.

Putting up her hands, she braced herself and only the sure knowledge of how recently a knife had been driven through his chest kept her from shoving him away. Was he truly healed? The very last time she'd seen him, the scar remained violent, and angry.

He'd waved off her concern then, assuring her his physicians told him everything was fine. Caged against him, she hated her reaction—which included the desperate desire to purr, rub her face to his shirt, and soak up his scent. "Sebastian, please..."

"No, this time you will listen. All of that...*nonsense* about the parties and the women? Those were appearances and have nothing to do with us. You and I are why we work. Yes, it has been a trial of a year, but we're together and we're here..."

Gaping, she stared up at him. "It isn't nonsense, Sebastian. We *don't* work."

"You keep saying we don't, but I don't believe it and neither do you." Then his mouth slammed down against hers, claiming and stealing every ounce of her breath. She fisted her hands and then she was lost to the lush, wet heat of his mouth as he slid his tongue along the seam of her lips. The request layered into the demand undid her. She threaded her arms around his neck and tumbled over the precipice.

Fire blasted through her, shattering every reservation, and she wanted more. God, she needed more. She'd missed him so damn much. As if he sensed her need, he gentled the kiss and his searing claim branded her. When he lifted his head and stared down at her, she swallowed, touching tentative fingers to the shadow of stubble on his jaw.

The mask he'd worn since she arrived slipped. Exhaustion and worry shone in his grave eyes. "Let me love you?" he asked and she melted.

Insanity, but then it had always been insanity with them from their first meeting—and the passion. Lord, the passion turned incendiary. She'd never experienced anything like it with anyone but Bastian. Madness to even consider his request, but she wasn't considering it at all. The moment his mouth closed over hers, she'd already surrendered.

She needed the connection, needed him. Rising on her tiptoes, she kissed him. He dragged her closer and then lifted her. "Yes, Bastian," she said against his mouth and felt, more than heard, his ragged sigh as he began striding down the hall. She forgot about the other people in the house, the island, the fight—everything.

There was only Bastian.

CHAPTER 5
SEBASTIAN

S ebastian didn't slow his step as he carried the very sensual, willing Meredith up the stairs and to his suite. Blessing the discretion of the staff as they vacated the hallway even while he strode down it, he lowered her only long enough to open the door and then they were inside. Turning, he pressed her against the wall and engaged the lock.

She fisted his shirt, and he stilled. Was she planning to push him away? But then she tugged at the buttons with a hint of impatience and eased his discord. He broke from the kiss and drank in the sight of her. A wealth of emotion danced over her face in the short time since she arrived—aggravation, impatience, a hint of amusement, affection, and, worst of them all, fear.

Yet the deep, nut brown of her eyes only revealed passion burning away the gut-wrenching anguish he'd fought for days. His Meredith was here and she was in his arms. When his shirt was opened, she pushed it off and he released her long enough to strip the fabric away and let it drop. Tangling his fingers in her hair, he stole another kiss.

He wanted to be gentle, but it was hard and raw and filled with the hurt of their separation. Distance and time meant nothing, not when he knew he *would* see her again. The fact she'd nearly robbed them of any future together, roused a fury in him like he'd never experienced before. When her tongue tangled with his and she shuddered, he groaned and pressed up against her.

A bite of pain on his shoulders encouraged the wild need racing through his veins. Taking what precious little of his control remained, he broke the kiss and stripped her clothes with an almost ruthless focus.

"Bastian..." The breathy whisper snagged his attention and he zeroed his gaze in on her face. He refused to miss anything. Her eyes widened and she touched two gentle fingers to his cheek, but she said nothing. Instead, she closed the distance and brushed her lips to his. He lowered his head, meeting the tender yearning in her kiss. So sweet and soft, it threatened to break him.

One hand flat against the wall, he drank in the soothing touch and let it leash the fierceness consuming him inside. He'd nearly lost her and he didn't understand the reasons why. God help him he would find out—he would fix it. He could not lose her.

His jaw clenched and, with regret, he freed

himself from the butterfly kisses seducing his soul. The violent need to claim her until she understood who she belonged to warred with the equally insistent drive to protect her from what belonging to him meant. The stroke of her fingers to his shoulders, then along the corded muscles of his arms and back again, left ribbons of fire. They threaded through him until his cock seemed to pulse in time with his heartbeat.

"I need you to be naked," he said and took a step back. If he kept touching her, he'd strip her bare and take her right there against the wall. Meredith's chest rose and fell, her creamy breasts straining against the sheer lace of her bra. Her blouse was wide open. "Take off the rest of your clothes, beautiful."

Thank God his voice didn't betray his shaken soul or the crushing desire threatening to overwhelm his judgment. When she bit her lower lip and sucked it between her teeth, he wanted to groan. The things he could do with her mouth— had done and would do again.

He'd been in hell without her. He descended there every time they said goodbye and only the sure knowledge they *would* be together sustained him. Impatience crawled through him as she remained against the wall and what looked like indecision flickered in her eyes.

Just when he thought the distance would tear him in two, she straightened and stripped off her blouse. A lazy smile curved her pink lips and her gaze fastened to his, pinning him in place. One article of clothing at a time drifted to land on the floor until she stood there, beautifully bare and resplendent—a goddess.

His goddess.

When he extended a hand to her, she rewarded him by twining her delicate fingers with his and the brutal ache in his chest eased. Drawing her to him, he cupped her face and bent to take her mouth. He intended to be as soft and tender as she'd been, but when she opened to him, the chain he'd fastened on himself shattered.

Wrapping his arms around her, he crushed her to him and surrendered to his relentless addiction for Meredith Blake. They went down on the bed together, and he flipped her onto her back. Devouring the pleasure in her kiss, he poured everything he felt for her into the contact. Her nipples pebbled against his chest and the longing to touch them, caress, and tease them had him abandoning her mouth.

Meredith threw her head back and groaned when he locked his lips around one dusky nipple. Her nails caressing his scalp encouraged him, and her body writhed as he blazed a wet trail to her other nipple to lavish it with the same treatment. The woman possessed perfect breasts—full, lush, and perfect for squeezing, playing. He bit down lightly on the heavy curve of one.

She shuddered and he glanced up to see her eyes fluttering closed. Her mouth opened and an abandoned moan vibrated through her. He brushed his fingers across her abdomen, aware of every ripple in her muscles. She melted to his touch and he adored pushing her until she lost any semblance of the patient professor.

In his bed, they broke the molds life crafted for them. Tweaking her taut nipple, he grinned at her gasp and then indulged himself in a long, slow exploration of her body. He knew every curve, every angle, every freckle—of which she possessed five—as well as the most darling of birthmarks. Reminded, he continued down to her hip and nuzzled the strawberry shaped mark.

But this close to her pussy, he forgot about playing and eased her thighs apart. The raw demand in his soul to take her might have receded under her embrace, but he wanted to taste her. She drove him mad with her soft sounds. The moment he glided his tongue along her clit, her gasp turned into a whimpering cry urging him on. Craving her release nearly as much as his own, he laved at the swollen bud until she arched off the bed forcing him to hold her in place. The buck of her hips drove him and he was merciless in his attention. She came with a sharp cry, and then collapsed.

Rising, he stripped off his slacks and stared down at her. Her eyelids were half-closed and pleasure transformed her expression. The heat of her gaze licked him and his hands shook by the time he retrieved a condom. For a moment, retreat flickered in her passion-drenched eyes and his chest tightened.

No, she wasn't allowed to leave him—not here, not anywhere, never again. He would not let her go. He would show her why they needed to be together, why he wanted her. Something of what he was feeling had to reflect in his expression, because Meredith's eyes widened. She pushed up on her elbows, the tousle of her dark blonde hair clinging to the dampness of her skin.

Unable to tolerate the separation, he slid back onto the bed and Meredith's arms came around him—thank God—welcoming him. Her mouth opened to his kiss. He poured all of his craving, heat, and primal desire for her into his kiss and gripped her hair tight.

His cock settled against her then her hand wrapped around him. He lifted obediently, letting her guide him to her slick, wet heat. Then he surged inside of her and she gasped against his mouth. She was so tight and, at the last moment, he managed to regain some semblance of control. It had been a long time—months—and he needed to slow down, to not hurt her.

But his impatient woman didn't allow him to extend their tumble into madness. She scissored her legs around his hips and rose up until he was buried to the hilt. Her mouth dropped open and her face went a deep pink. The flames were back in her eyes when he broke the kiss, but she nipped his jaw and then dug her nails into his back. Sweat beaded on his forehead.

He wanted to slam inside of her, thrust until they were both blind with pleasure, but he had to know, needed to be sure. "Are you okay?" The words were harsh and rode shallow pants of air as though his lungs couldn't fully expand.

"Yes." She dug her nails into his back and

flexed her thighs against his hips. "Oh dear God, yes—Bastian..." The sensual need punctuating the words gave him permission. He thrust in short, swift motions while tangling his tongue with hers.

She went taut with tension and her inner muscles clamped down around him so hard. He fought the climax screaming through him, but her cries against his mouth pushed him over. He pistoned his hips, desperate to follow her. The plunge caught him off guard, sharp and violent. He came as she convulsed around him with only the ragged pant of their breathing and the slippery wet slide of their skin on skin to accompany them.

The orgasm left him drained and he collapsed against her, content to bask in her sweet embrace. Quivers raced over her. She clung to him and pressed kisses to his face and then to his jaw.

She was there and in his arms. Yet, his contentment seemed edged in something he couldn't quite define. He wasn't even sure he wanted to. Burying his face against her neck, he nuzzled the spot above her rapidly beating pulse. Shoving the concern to the back of his mind, he eased away from her.

Her breathing slowed, and he angled his head to check. Her eyes closed, her mouth curved in a hint of a satisfied smile—sound asleep. The dark smudges beneath her eyes told him she was exhausted from the moment he'd seen her.

With a gentle finger, he traced the shadows. It was his job to erase those, to make her safe and secure so she wouldn't worry again. He had no idea how he would accomplish it, but by God he would do it. Rising, he stepped into the bathroom to deal with the condom. Afterward, he came back to the bed. She hadn't stirred. Drawing the covers up, he slid in beside her and drew her boneless form to him.

To his delight, she relaxed against his touch and snuggled. It was the middle of the day, but he hadn't slept well in the near week since her phone call. Still, even with her there, sleep proved elusive.

An uncomfortable emotion lodged in his chest and he settled for stroking her hair and watching her. When she woke, they would talk. It didn't matter how long it took, but even his determination didn't diminish his unease.

~

MEREDITH

Her muscles were languid, yet the quiet ache of soreness invaded her sleep. She didn't want to wake up and burrowed deeper into the warmth along her side. Exhaustion left her worn down and keeping her eyes closed meant keeping the rest of the world at bay. When her pillow shifted, she mumbled a protest and rubbed her cheek against a...very hot, masculine chest. Reality invaded like an icy splash of water.

Lifting her head, she found Sebastian's black gaze studying her. The memory of losing herself in his arms flooded through her, shoving away the last traces of drowsiness. "It wasn't a dream," she murmured and even the thought made her smile. She'd enjoyed vivid dreams of him before, but nothing like what they'd shared.

"Hello." He cupped the back of her head and she obeyed his silent request to meet the slow, soul-searing kiss he gave her.

"Hi," she whispered against his mouth. Nuzzling her nose to his, she shivered and he tightened his arms before dragging the sheet up to wrap it around her. The action made her want to sigh all over again. He'd thought her cold. The gentleness in his actions and the warmth of his breath on her cheek threatened to pull her apart. "How long was I asleep?"

"Not long." He combed his fingers through her hair, soothing the quiet alarm jangling along her nerves. "Feel better?"

Yes. Better and worse, but she couldn't quite sort through all the emotions bubbling inside. Still wrestling with her response, she feathered her fingers across his chest and down his side. The puckered ridge of skin beneath her fingertips catapulted her from her indecision.

Sitting up, she ignored the sheet dropping to pool around her waist or the familiar and welcome weight of his hand gliding over her hip. The scar transected his side, the skin paler than the ruddy tan he'd earned through hours spent in the sun. Thankfully, the skin was cool to the touch— not the angry, hot slash the one and only other time she'd been near enough to see the damage.

Sebastian caught her wrist as she traced her finger along the ridged skin. "You don't need to worry..." he began in the sinful, European accent that turned her muscles to butter.

"Did it hurt badly?" Dammit, she should have been there. Who'd looked after him? Who'd made sure he took his medicine and rested? Sebastian loved to play, and he was so active. He'd taken her skiing, scuba diving, and once—God help her —he'd even taken her skydiving. The horror of those moments free falling left her nearly drunk by the time they'd touched down.

"Not terribly, no." He let go of her wrist and stroked her arm. Meredith never wondered why women flocked to him. Handsome as sin, charming as hell, and he possessed an almost carefree personality that enchanted nearly everyone who met him. She was hardly an exception to the rule, but what sealed the deal for her was his eyes.

Lifting her head, she sought the deep black of his gaze now. Something in his eyes captivated her from their first harried meeting. "Really?" The scar was nearly two inches in length and nearly a half-inch thick. It transected his side and lay right between two ribs—the blade had cut clean into him. Trembling seized her and her throat went dry.

He sat up, pulled her into his lap and she buried her face against his throat. Crooning a low, soothing note, he rubbed her back. "Really." Then, with a sigh, he continued. "Injuries, particularly shocking ones, don't hurt nearly as much as you might think. The mind protects itself, or at least my doctors said it did. Why else would I have broken my leg twice in my life or fractured my ribs who knows how many times?"

A watery laugh inched up inside of her at his droll tone. "I wish I'd been there."

"I don't." The swift disagreement struck her like a slap. His arms tightened around her. "I make for the most miserable of patients, or so the staff tells me." The lighthearted jibe didn't ease the sting. When she shivered, he rubbed his hands up and down her spine. "You're still cold. Are you feeling okay?"

Swallowing the lump of misery along with what was left of her pride, Meredith summoned up a smile and pulled away. "I'm tired. And I wouldn't mind a shower..."

"I bet you're hungry, too." He caressed her cheek. "I'll send down for your bags and food. We can make a picnic of it. Hmm, on second thought, maybe I'll just send down for the food. I like the idea of dining al fresco."

A blush heated her skin at the blatant sensuality in his voice. "I really don't think I want to be bare-assed nude when anyone on your staff comes in...and I thought we could eat downstairs. Maybe on the pretty patio..."

Bastian followed her off the bed and wrapped his arms around her, drawing her to him and he nuzzled a kiss to neck. "Let me tell you a secret. Outside of this room, there are a lot of people. If we step out, we have to spend time with them. I'd rather not share you with anyone."

A part of her thrilled at the possessiveness in his romantic declaration, but hiding behind closed doors didn't appeal to her. She hesitated and Bastian turned her around and kissed her, the claiming in his action curling her toes and kindling a fresh wave of heat. He growled, and his grin turned playful. "Go shower, darling, but take your time so I can join you."

He grabbed his pants and shirt and, by the time she reached the bathroom door, he'd stepped out of the room. Meredith let out a breath she hadn't realized she'd been holding. Stepping right up to the porcelain countertop, she braced her hands against it and stared at herself in the mirror. From her tousled hair to her kiss-swollen lips, she looked like she'd just rolled out of bed.

How was it possible they'd ended up there? Her stomach clenched at the memory. Why couldn't she tell him all the thoughts in her head? What held her tongue every single time? Glancing back into the bedroom, she spotted the disheveled sheets and sighed. She tingled everywhere he'd touched her. All she had to do was close her eyes and the memory of his caresses swept over her.

Only a few hours since she'd struggled desperately to get him out of her mind. To let go of what could never be. Yet, here she was, craving heating her blood. She knew the moment he slid into the shower with her—hell, who was she kidding? If he looked at her she'd want him again. Sebastian Dagmar, prince and Grand Duke of the

Andraste dynasty, turned her brains to mush and liquefied her intelligence.

He'd just said he was glad she hadn't been with him, implying it wasn't her place. Despite being hundreds of miles from the press, he didn't want her to leave the room.

Maybe he just wants to be with me? She turned away from the mirror, unwilling to look at the pathetic gleam in her own eyes.

She switched on the shower and, while the water heated, retrieved an unopened toothbrush left on the counter—for her. Staring at the packaging, she sighed. He'd made all the arrangements. Of course he'd used Andraste influence or someone else's to coax the university. He'd sent Kate to do the negotiations, make the travel arrangements, and lured her halfway around the world. Every detail, from her travel visas to her leave from the university, smoothed flawlessly and they'd even set out a toothbrush.

And why wouldn't they? She was a sure thing. After brushing her teeth, she slid under the pounding of the hot water and bent her head. *He did go to so much trouble, and he said he wanted to see me. That has to count for something, doesn't it?* She so longed to believe it, but did she want to believe it because it was true or because *I'm a mistress and I'm in love.*

What the hell was she going to do?

CHAPTER 6
SEBASTIAN

Meredith puzzled him. Her concentrated frown on the gardens sprawling beyond the windows was not the expression he'd expected. But then nothing she'd done since arriving on St. Christos followed presumed convention or her normal behavior. Truthfully, nothing she'd done since she'd called him in Los Angeles matched what he knew of her. He felt her withdrawal and it was far more than physical. Sometime between her shower and his return, she'd erected an emotional wall between them.

He hated it. Maybe the wall was why he couldn't quite keep his hands to himself and why he'd angled his chair to crowd into her space.

"You're staring at me." She picked up her coffee cup and cut a sideways look at him. The corners of her eyes crinkled, but it was tension, not amusement.

"I like looking at you." He spoke bluntly. A blush pinkened her cheeks and he smiled. Candor

99

was rare in his life. His every statement had to be vetted for potential impact, but he'd never felt the need to censor himself with Meredith. He disliked intensely the sensation he should begin. Catching a lock of her hair, he smoothed the strands between his thumb and forefinger.

She laughed and set the mug down, turning her attention to him finally. "You're impossible."

"I assure you, for you, I am infinitely possible."

Her gaze locked on his, searching, and he willed for her to find what she needed. A wordless pulse raced through him, a need so visceral and base it assaulted the very core of his civility. He understood why monarchs of old locked their women up where no one else could get to them. It wasn't a lack of trust or faith, merely a desire to possess.

God, he wanted to possess Meredith. Every thought, every moment of every day. He wanted to stamp his ownership so clearly no one would dare touch her. Yet doing so painted a target on her, and he'd learned a brutal truth by watching Anna's life upend because he'd made a phone call to force his brother's hand.

"And now you're scowling." Meredith almost sighed and Sebastian fought to get his emotions back into check, smoothing over his face. The last thing he wanted was to push her away. "Bastian—"

"Meredith." He nearly spoke over her and bit back his next words. "Please...go on."

She paused, studying him. "It's all right, you were about to say something."

Accepting the invitation, he shifted in his seat and caught her hand in his. The warm satin of her skin as enticing as it was comforting. He never tired of touching her. "I know we have issues, and perhaps I haven't been the most accessible of late, but I want to repair any injury between us."

It was a testament to his self-control that he didn't pick her up and take her back to bed. There, at least, he knew exactly how to please her. If he drowned her in pleasure, she might reconsider the notion of leaving him altogether.

When she didn't outright reject his statement, he pressed on. "I want to spend time with you and get it right. I know we bent the truth to get you here."

"If you define bent as lied then, yes, you did." Did he detect a trace of a smile in her voice? The corners of her mouth twitched, but it was the gleam of humor in her eyes which ultimately betrayed her.

"Very well, I lied. I cheated. I facilitated fraud in order to secure your time for a few days." Considering it was only a small portion of what he was willing to do to get her to see him, he saw no reason to avoid admitting it.

"And you're not remotely sorry, are you?" Despite the implied chastisement, her eyes continued to warm.

"No." He shook his head. "Not in the slightest.

You are *here*. This—us together—was and is the goal."

"Hmm." She reached for her coffee mug and glanced at the grounds. "It's impossible to be angry with you, even when I am."

A grin tugged at the corners of his mouth. "So I am forgiven for the charade?"

"Well, I wouldn't go that far." But the smile she'd been fighting began to break free. "I really did want to do the project. Return Times are a fascinating challenge."

"Then I'll make sure you do it. Daniel really seemed fascinated by the whole idea." Hell, he'd finance a hundred puzzles for her to solve.

"Daniel?" Her smile faltered.

"Voldakov—"

"The owner of Spherecast." Meredith warmed considerably and, for the first time since they'd sat down to eat, she leaned toward him. "Did you know he actually developed an algorithm based on one of my papers?"

"Did he?" Captivated by the excitement reflected in her eyes, he fought the surge of irrational jealousy. The mention of Daniel put the light into her eyes. *Daniel. Another man.*

"Yes." She laughed, a giddy sound, and the tension stiffening her spine went loose. "It was all very fascinating, but he applied one of my theories to a program he was building. It uses base algorithms to identify information chunks and reconstruct an entire server's worth of data based on stringing data theory which presupposes individual chunking of data bits will have similar bases. Then, by identifying the primary numbers and matching, you should be able to reconstruct a problem by piecing together the solution. It was a delightful challenge."

Enthusiasm shimmered in every word, her face warmed, and pure delight rippled in her laugh. "Of course, application and theory are wholly different beasts and we maintained a regular correspondence during his software build so he could get my input on troubleshooting."

"I didn't know you were involved in his work." He hadn't. Of course, it explained Daniel's excitement when Sebastian mentioned Meredith. "What other projects have you done?"

"A few. A lot of my work is theoretical, but there are people out there who see beyond the numbers. More than one company has approached me with a proprietary interest." She settled back in the chair and played with his fingers.

Pleased by the contact, he allowed himself the pleasure of stroking his thumb against the side of her hand. "You believe information should be in the public domain." Of this, he was absolutely certain. In fact, her belief and speech on the subject had actually been the source of their very first debate.

"You remembered?" Why did it surprise her? The haze of pleasure in her eyes sent a jolt through him.

"Of course I do. I remember everything about the night we met. You wore a cream dress. It was perfectly understated and hugged your curves so well I was envious of it." It had been a boring, obsequious event. One which held no interest for him, but he'd attended because Armand was in the process of launching a series of clinics and refused to reschedule for an event which only required a family face to be seen.

"That dress. Lord, I'd almost forgotten about the dress." She covered her mouth and her face went a deeper pink, but her eyes darkened with arousal.

"I loved how you looked in it," he told her, perfectly aware of where her thoughts went. "I loved how you looked when I ripped it off you even more." In their enthusiasm, they'd been too impatient to take the time when the zipper jammed. Meredith laughed and he lifted their joined hands to his lips and kissed her knuckles.

"I thought for sure I would have to return to my room in a towel. You didn't even leave my panties intact." Her eyes widened.

Still grinning at the memory, he shrugged. "You didn't need clothes for the next several hours."

"Hours? Try days. Three days we stayed in your suite. I didn't know how I would ever explain to my department head why I'd missed so many of the conference lectures. Thank God they recorded all of them." She laughed.

"We were having fun," he told her, sobering. "Stay with me, and let's find that fun again—you and I."

Her amusement shifted to thoughtful consideration. "I don't know if we can. We're not those people anymore."

"Yes, we are," he argued, cupping her face and pressing his forehead to hers. "We are exactly who we were then. I am still as crazy for you today as I was the night we met. In fact, I'm showing great restraint by not stripping you naked and having you for breakfast."

Her breath hitched at the declaration. "Sex has never been our problem, but it can't be the basis for a relationship."

"Why not?" Their conversation was too important. She was too important. "Do you know how many relationships out there simply make do? We work, you and me. I can be myself with you, no pretenses. I know it hasn't been easy, and I don't pretend to understand everything you've gone through, but I *need* you, Meredith. Stay with me. Give me these next few days. I promise, you won't regret it."

They needed time together, time to repair the damage of the last year. He'd kept her at arm's length while he recovered. Not his first choice, and one he recognized as a mistake. He'd reasoned it was to protect her, which was true, to a point.

She sighed and tugged her hand from his. Rising, Meredith paced to the glass and folded her arms, staring out into the garden. Though she'd been the one to pull away, she looked so alone and forlorn he couldn't stay in his chair. Moving behind her, he wrapped his arms around her and cradled her against his chest.

"I know I'm asking for a lot." And if taking his pride in hand to beg would help, well, he would.

"Oh Bastian..." She sighed and closed her eyes, leaning her head back against his shoulder. It wasn't capitulation, not yet. Her brow creased with a frown, and she bit at her lip. She hadn't surrendered, but she considered it. "How does this even work? We're not going to solve anything hiding away in your room."

They weren't hiding, but he let it go for the moment and concentrated on her question. "We spend time together. We talk about what is important to you, what is important to me. We get to know each other again..." Remember what drew them together in the first place because, though his feelings were far from waning, maybe hers had.

It kicked him square in the gut to consider the possibility, but she lived an entire life he wasn't part of—a career she was proud of and work she thrived on. Loosening his grip, he coaxed her to turn. "Maybe you could even explain your last paper to me, the one on class polynomials."

"The research was only released last month." Disbelief warred with surprise and she gave him a wondering look. "How did you know about my paper?"

"I have every paper you've ever published and subscriptions to all the major journals." Needing to prove the point, he kissed the tip of her nose and took her hand, tugging her gently. "Come."

His briefcase was downstairs in the office he used when he was on the island. He hadn't planned to do any work whatsoever, but with Meredith in tow, he led the way down the staircase, past the open drawing room and reception hall, to a private hallway. Armand's office was also located in the same section and, though another was reserved for George, his youngest brother never darkened the doorway of his.

At the entrance to the dark-wood paneled room, Bastian had to release her in order to open the double doors. Inside, he was gratified when she not only let him take her hand again, but threaded her fingers through his. Guiding her across the room, he paused at the oversized cherry wood desk and unlocked his briefcase with a three-digit combination.

"913." Meredith's little gasp dragged his attention to her. Tears shimmered in her eyes.

"Yes." He gave her a small smile. "I told you, I remember everything." 913 was his suite number. He'd discovered the best woman in the world behind those doors. Sentimental perhaps, but he considered it his lucky number.

She sniffed then gave him a smile that threatened to stop his heart. When she leaned into him, her breasts brushed his arm and her fingers tightened against his. "Okay," she whispered, her voice husky and soft. "I am pretty sure this isn't what you dragged me down here to see."

It took him a moment to even remember why they'd come to his office. Dropping his gaze to her lips, he gave into temptation and bent his head to kiss her. The moment their mouths brushed, electricity sizzled in his nervous system and threatened to short-circuit his brain. Leashing the raging desire firing in his blood, he lifted his head and stared into her eyes. "No, the briefcase isn't what I wanted to show you."

The corners of her eyes crinkled and she laughed. "You take my breath away."

"Ditto," he told her solemnly and forced himself to open the case and pull out the journal of the American Mathematical Society. He held it up for her inspection. "See, I read everything you do."

Her mouth went slack and her earlier tears threatened again, one splashing down her cheek. "Why?"

"Why what, darling?" He hated her tears, hated them. He wanted to make them go away.

"If you—this...why do you read everything I write?"

Did she truly not understand?

Sebastian slid into a chair and tugged her into his lap, giving into the desire he'd been struggling with since he'd seen her again to enfold her close. He wanted her near always. "Because you wrote it. You." It really summed up everything for him.

Meredith stared down at the journal and then up at him. She was wavering.

"Say yes, Meredith." It was a calculated risk, ordering her. She could still tell him no. "Say you'll stay. Say you'll give me these few days. I know we can make this work."

Closing her eyes, she bowed her head, but she didn't pull away. If anything she moved closer and fisted his shirt in her hand. "Do you really think we can?" Hope and longing so mirroring his own twined in her question.

"I know we can," he told her, resolved. "Say. Yes."

She opened her eyes, brought her face to his and kissed him. He welcomed the slow, tentative invasion of her tongue and tangled his hand in her hair. Kissing her was an erotic pleasure. He indulged his senses, lapping up the taste of her sweetness while reveling in how she bloomed to his touch.

"Say yes," he told her between long, strokes of his tongue against hers. When she finally broke the kiss and lifted her head, he experienced the weight of her study all the way to his bones.

Whatever she'd seen must have satisfied her because she exhaled with a beaming smile. "Yes."

"Yes?" Relief flooded him.

"Yes," she repeated and then laughed when he crushed her close. "Yes, Bastian. Yes."

Time. She'd given him time. *Thank God.*

~

MEREDITH

Still in his lap, she shifted to claim the journal issue, which had included the title of her research on the cover. Sebastian rested one hand on her hip and massaged her nape with the other. First his insistence they could work this out, then the combination lock to his briefcase—the number of the suite where they'd ended up spending three hedonistic days in total lust with each other —then the journal. Her emotions seesawed all over the place.

"Where did you go?" Sebastian's quiet question tugged her from the memory of their first weekend.

"Vienna," she smiled. "I was thinking about the conference. The dinner. What happened after the dinner."

Wickedness deepened his smile. "I still think they could have given us a better wine selection."

Laughter erupted through her and she shook her head. "You harangued our poor waiter until he went and brought you a bottle."

"I was trying to impress a lady," he admitted. "Cheap wine was not going to cut it."

"You were not." She tried to laugh it off, but when he lifted his brows and stared at her with utter sobriety, her amusement faded.

"I most certainly was." He slid his fingers up into her hair and began to massage her scalp. The touch was downright hypnotic and the tension beading her muscles since she'd walked in to shower began to ease.

"Why?" The man commanded attention when he walked into a room. She'd only seen him in passing, following a panel where she'd engaged in a heated disagreement with an economist. The man cited her dissertation in his presentation and misrepresented her findings. She'd been livid by the time he finished. She'd intended to address the situation privately—and then he'd called on her.

Sebastian's brows climbed. "Because you were the most beautiful woman in the room—and the most intelligent—and even after bribing someone to switch out the dining cards so I could be seated next to you, you barely noticed I was there."

It was her turn to gape. "Of course I knew you were there. Everyone at the table stood and Doctor Ramanijun nearly had a heart attack when I didn't stand along with everyone else. Wait—you bribed someone to sit at our table?"

He continued to massage her scalp and, even as she leaned into the touch, he traced the shell of her ear with his lips. The lightest of kisses, it sent heat radiating along every nerve. "Oh, yes. I'd seen this vibrant, passionate woman argue quite brilliantly earlier in the day and I wanted to meet her. They'd seated you too far away for my liking. Then you were more interested in the septuage-narian than me. I had to do something."

Uncertain whether she was more shocked he'd been trying to impress her or the fact he'd bribed his way onto her table, Meredith fumbled for words. She settled for a helpless, "But why?" *Why go to all that trouble?* For her? Because she'd gotten angry with someone?

Sebastian caught her earlobe and tugged on it. A pulse in her belly echoed his touch. She drowned in sensation whenever they were to-gether. He really was the only man she'd ever met who could get her mind to shut down. In fact, after all their years together, she'd learned his nearness greatly impeded her ability to puzzle through a problem.

It took her a moment to realize he'd stopped and considered her with a frown. Her system was so haywire, she floundered for what put the dark look on his face.

"You really don't know, do you?"

The disbelief in his voice brought her back to earth. "No," she admitted, even though her face flamed. "I'm nobody."

His mouth compressed into a thin line and his expression hardened. Even his black eyes seemed to glaze over with a fierce kind of ice. "Don't ever talk about yourself in those terms again. You are *more* than somebody. You're the most beautiful, vibrant, alive woman I've ever met. You are not coy about pleasure or dislike and you take such joy out of the simplest things. You are also brilliant and your mind fascinates me like no other." He tapped the journal still in her hands. "I read these because I want to comprehend all the facets. I want to be a part of it even in some small way. Do not ever call yourself nothing. You are somebody, Meredith Blake. You're a professor, a teacher, a researcher, a gifted doctor of mathematics, a daughter, a friend—and you're *mine.*"

If his statement hadn't already robbed her of speech, he claimed her mouth in a kiss that branded her all the way to her soul. The journal slipped out of her hands and she gripped his shoulders. He sought entry to her mouth with his tongue and she welcomed him. Emotions detonated inside of her and his fierce declaration left her defenseless.

He cupped her breast and her nipples tightened even as her belly went low and taut. Digging her fingers into his shirt, she'd barely pulled two buttons open when a knock sounded at the door.

Sebastian growled—actually growled—and lifted his head. "Go away." Order delivered, he captured her open mouth in another wet kiss and the interruption slid away as she ran her palms across the hot skin of his chest.

The knock repeated, but Sebastian ignored it. When it came a third time, he dragged his head back and turned a look so primal and fierce on the door, she prayed she'd never be on the receiving end of it. "What?" he demanded. When she would have scrambled off his lap, he tightened his grip on her, refusing to allow her escape.

"Please forgive the intrusion, sir, but your brother needs to speak with you immediately." Vidal's announcement lanced the bubble of passion and Sebastian swore, colorfully she imagined, in Norwegian. At least she thought it was Norwegian.

Vidal, wisely, didn't respond to Sebastian's epithets. Meredith bit her lip, and tried to get her ragged breathing under control. Pressing a kiss as gentle as his expression was not to her lips, Sebastian murmured, "Forgive me, I have to take his call, but I will make it quick."

She started to ease off his lap, but he once

again tightened his grip and frowned at her before plucking the phone up from the desk. He greeted his brother in the same language he'd sworn in. The cool, smoothness of his voice belied his temper so perfectly, if she hadn't witnessed the transformation she'd never have known he was upset in the first place. Though she couldn't make out the words, she heard the deep timbre of his brother's voice muted as it was by the phone. It held a similar cadence and accent to Sebastian's.

"When?" Urgency punctuated the word and Sebastian's mouth tightened. He glanced at her, and she could almost read the regret in his expression as he gave her a gentle tap. Understanding the request, she slid off his lap and stood with his assistance. He ran a hand up her arm and caressed her cheek before circling the desk. "I'm going to my computer right now. How certain is Peterson?"

Standing behind his desk, one hand palm down as he stared at his computer, he looked commanding. But it was the tousled dark hair and the broad expanse of his chest revealed by the several opened buttons on his shirt, which transformed his command into something more primal and masculine.

"No," Sebastian said. "It's loading now."

Meredith glanced away from him, vividly aware of every breath he took. Scooping up the journal from the floor, she set it on the desk and stroked her finger across the cover to trace his name on the subscription label. *Sebastian Dag-*

mar. He subscribed just so he could read her papers. She'd never made a big deal out of being published. In fact, she'd only mentioned it in passing a handful of times if she recalled correctly—one time specifically because he'd taken her skiing and she'd needed to finish reading the final copy before it went to print.

It seemed to lend an even greater import to his actions. Awareness of his regard kept her peeking at him from behind the fall of her bangs. He wasn't speaking, but she could still hear the murmur of his brother's words. Staring at him only fanned the flames of need he'd lit with his kisses, so she forced herself to look away.

"Impossible." Sebastian's impatience ratcheted up with every syllable. He paused. "I said it was impossible..." and he switched languages between one word and the next. Whatever their topic, it was private. She suddenly felt very self-conscious standing in the middle of his office with her blouse open to her navel.

Glancing away, she began to button it up as casually as possible. One entire wall of his office was comprised of bookshelves. Family pictures scattered amongst the books, along with a couple of model airplanes and a replica of Rodin's *The Thinker*.

The statue reminded her of their last trip to Paris and their midnight visit to the Musée Rodin. She mentioned she'd always wanted to see it and he'd whisked her away in a private car at one in the morning. They'd toured the whole exhibit with only Vidal for company—not even a docent insisted on going with them.

They'd spent a magical evening together. When she'd complained about her shoes and Sebastian insisted she take them off. She'd spent nearly a half hour just staring at the seminal piece, moved beyond words. Daring to run her finger over the man's tiny fist, she smiled at the memory and then investigated the photographs.

His brothers were prominent in them, as was a silver-haired woman she recognized as his mother. She'd seen the dowager princess once. Or rather, she'd seen her briefly. They'd attended an opera in New York, a very hurried affair—a car picked her up and zipped her to the city. She'd met him at a hotel and he'd surprised her with tickets.

It was one of his favorites, he'd told her, and they'd entered the theater through a private entrance and taken equally private stairs to a box. The opera proved a wonderful experience. During the intermission, she'd excused herself to go to the restroom. When she'd returned, Sebastian had been in a discussion with the woman, and bid her farewell without introducing her to Meredith.

Meredith hadn't realized who the woman was, not until later. It was the first time the reality of her place in Sebastian's life settled in—of course one didn't introduce the mistress to the mother.

He'd gone very quiet behind her. She glanced over to find his tense expression focused on the computer screen. She really should leave him to the discussion with his brother and stop snooping through his things before she tossed the fresh chance they were taking to her own insecurities.

She had the door half-opened when he spoke again. "Meredith?"

Glancing back, she gave him a quick smile. "It's all right, talk to your brother. I'm going to take a walk and cool off." She meant it to be playful, but it came out tighter and a little more fraught than lighthearted. Riding the emotional seesaw left her unbalanced.

"You don't have to—"

But she waved him off. He'd switched to a foreign language for a reason and she wasn't offended at all. Everyone deserved the right to a private conversation. Closing the door as quietly as she'd opened it, she glanced up and down the length of the hall. Maybe a walk in the garden beneath his room would give her a chance to clear her head and sort out her muddled thoughts.

Choosing the direction of the open reception hall and sitting room, she found the door—and a lot more people than she'd realized were in residence. A maid polished the tables and a guard stood just inside the door. Both nodded to her politely when she made eye contact and, when she hesitated, the man at the door gave her an inquiring look.

"I don't suppose you can tell me where the garden is?" she asked.

"Are you planning to go outside, ma'am?"

It was an odd response. *Why else would she be asking where the garden was?* "Yes, Basti—er—His Highness is on the phone. I thought I would get some air." *They'd let her go outside, wouldn't they?*

"Of course, ma'am. If you'll give me a moment?" He touched a finger to his ear. "Miss Blake is stepping outside to take some air. She requires an escort."

She most certainly did not. "I'm perfectly capable of—"

"Meredith." Terry's greeting threw her lifeline, and she spun around to find him approaching from another hallway.

"You're still here." Guilt-flavored-relief swamped her. She'd all but forgotten Terry and his possibly precarious position thanks to defending her during her mad reunion with Sebastian.

"Of course." He gave her a questioning smile. "Gerard said you wanted to take a walk outside."

"I do and I don't really need an escort." However, if they required her to have one, at least it was someone she knew.

"Well how about a friend, then?" He kept his tone light and gestured toward the sitting room. "The doors are right there."

Nodding gratefully, she followed him to French doors that opened onto a wide, stone veranda. The entire house was surrounded by a wide expanse of green and fresh air touched with a hint of salt wrapped around her as soon as she stepped outside. Steps led down from the veranda toward the garden, a wild profusion of colors decorated the garden with roses being the most prominent. Someone took very good care of it and, while she knew next to nothing about gardening, she knew what she liked.

Not slowing, she kept going until she was completely out of the house and amidst the floral scents. Dragging the sweetness into her lungs, she paused and tilted her face up to the sun. She needed to calm the riot in her system.

When she'd broken up with Bastian, she believed it to be the right thing to do. But seeing him now—she couldn't imagine never seeing him again. So how the hell did she reconcile needing him and wanting him with the position she'd have to occupy to be with him?

"Meredith, are you all right?" Terry was right behind her, close enough for the sound of his voice to make her jump. "I'm sorry."

She was the one who should be sorry. Terry was her friend, and she kept forgetting he even existed. "I'm fine." She let out a shaky breath. "I just have a lot to think about." Being with Bastian made thinking impossible, but when it was the two of them—it always felt like it was just the two of them. All of his beautiful, powerful male force focused on her. He was a relentless addiction in her blood and, like any good addict, could she possibly make good choices when it came to him?

Terry touched her shoulder. "I'm sorry I didn't tell you where we were going."

"It's all right." She'd already forgiven him the

deception. At the end of the day, Bastian would have gotten his way with or without Terry's assistance. "You did tell me to turn the job down." Sebastian was his employer.

"Yeah, but I could have done more, especially if you didn't want to be here." He gave her a shoulder squeeze.

"Really, it's—"

"O'Connor, you can leave us now." Sebastian's voice cracked over the quiet and Terry's hand fell away from her. She turned to find Sebastian's dark brooding gaze locked on Terry until he backed up a pace.

"I'll be nearby if you need me, Meredith." Terry nodded to the edge of the garden, then inclined his head to Sebastian before walking away.

Once Terry was out of earshot, Meredith lifted her brows. "You were a little rude."

"He oversteps a *lot*." Sebastian answered curtly and closed the distance between them. "Why did you leave?"

"You were talking to your brother. I really didn't think you wanted to discuss family business in front of your mistress." Two could be tart, and she was tired of dancing around the topic. He didn't have the right to act all lord of the manor in one breath and become a coaxing lover in the next. The shifting behavior confused the hell out of her.

Sebastian's harsh expression changed to one of shock. She didn't think she'd ever seen him wear such a look before, but when he spoke, danger edged his words. "My *what*?"

CHAPTER 7
SEBASTIAN

Her words struck him like a physical blow and all the air whooshed out of him. His temper had never been a pretty thing—he'd always been more like mallet in comparison to Armand's scalpel. Due to that, he'd long endeavored to contain his reactions—to leash them lest his tempestuous emotions land him in scandals, per his father's advice.

The suggestion to rein in his reactions came after Sebastian damn near beat another boy bloody at boarding school. His title, his family's wealth, and his father's diplomatic skills smoothed the whole incident over. Months of lessons followed the episode, most of which took him most of his life to perfect, but he knew the part he played and he played it well.

The last several days—hell, the last several months—all weighed on him, beginning with the blade in the dark arranged by a supposed family friend and culminating in the phone call from the love of his life ending their relationship. He'd twisted himself into knots to keep his cool, to stay in control, and then she hit him with the most ridiculous charge.

"Your mistress. I'm not an idiot, Bastian. Let's not pretend, not at this juncture." She let out an exasperated huff. Color bloomed in her cheeks and temper fired the dark chocolate of her eyes, blasting him. "I know my place. You've made it perfectly clear. And I don't even care—no, scratch that, I *care*. Maybe I care too much, a reality made clear when I saw the story about your engagement. I know, you said it wasn't true and, okay, maybe it wasn't...this time—"

Red hazed over his vision, and a dull roar filled his ears. She bandied around words *like*, *maybe*, and the idea it wasn't true *this time*.

"I know we've agreed to give this time and decided we shouldn't talk of these things, but I'm an adult. I agreed to this relationship. I—" She fumbled and raked her hands through her hair. "I *want* to be what you need, but I don't know if I can anymore." The last came out on a note so forlorn, it cut him deeper than all the rest. His soul began to bleed.

Shoving his hands in his pockets, he fought the urge to yell. The rapid escalation of his temper eroded his control. Jaw clenched, he fought the immediate, visceral yell backing up in his lungs. *Focus on her words.* To create distance from the pain they evoked took every ounce of his will. He needed to address her concerns because, clearly, the chasm between them was littered with more than jagged rocks of misunderstanding.

"You are not my mistress." He had to keep his temper in check. Yelling at her would not serve him in this. *Rational.*

Stay rational.

The wind chose the same moment to pick up, whipping her hair up and away from her face. One aspect of Meredith which always attracted him was her absolute lack of artifice. She didn't wear cosmetics unless she had to. She rarely wore jewelry—just a watch her father gave her at graduation and a pair of diamond studs, tiny little chips, from her grandmother gifted to her for her eighteenth birthday. These facts fascinated him along with every gram of knowledge he'd devoured about her in all their years together. *Mistress...how can she possibly believe she's my mistress?*

Her nose wrinkled and her jaw tightened. He recognized the signs of her temper and he couldn't listen to another word of her argument. Not when she insulted him and herself in the same breath.

"Sebastian—"

"Be silent." He cut her off and, while it flew in the face of everything he believed and he'd never allow another to speak to her in the same tone, he needed to hold onto the rapidly fraying ends of his temper before he said something they would both regret. Stalking forward, he invaded her space and stared down at her. "You are *not* my mistress. Not now. Not ever. I do not pretend when I am with you..."

Her mouth opened then snapped shut again with a click of her teeth.

Satisfied when she elected to not interrupt him, he fisted his hands in his pockets. He wanted to drag her close and kiss her until he blasted the ludicrous idea out of her head, but it wouldn't address the problem. If the solution were so easy, they'd have already dealt with it. "I have *never* pretended when I am with you." With Meredith, he got to be the man, not the prince, and how the hell could she not know how precious she was to him? "And your place?" His breath hitched. "I don't even know what the hell that means. The only place I've ever wanted you is with me." Even then, he'd denied himself.

Mutiny shimmered in her eyes, but she only lifted her eyebrows in silent inquiry.

"Yes, please—answer." Frustration corded his muscles. He clenched his fists until two of his knuckles popped.

"One, don't ever tell me to *be silent* again." She didn't bother to disguise her quiet fury and, damn she was beautiful when riled. "Two, you never have to pretend with me? Good to know. I've only ever seen you behind closed doors where no one else can see you. Since I never get to be on your arm in a crowd, I wouldn't know how you behave socially, now would I? And, yes, I know you want me with you, but only *when* you want me, *where* you want me, and *how* you want. You make all the decisions. You—" Her voice cracked, pitching high for a moment. "*You* decide. You get hurt and I hear nothing for days, only a cryptic message passed from your *bodyguard* to Terry saying you were alive. I got one five-minute phone call and then nothing. I'm not an idiot," she repeated, as though she needed to illustrate the point. "For five years, Sebastian, five *years*, I've been your dirty little secret. Maybe that's enough for some women. Hell, maybe it was enough for me, but I want more than private assignations and stolen days."

Her words arrested him and she paused, releasing a shaky little laugh dipped in tears. "I want more." Spreading her arms, she lifted her shoulders in a helpless shrug. "I love you, but I can't do this anymore—"

She offered him heaven and hell rolled together. Forcing his fists to release, he dragged his hands from his pockets and caught her arms. "Meredith, you're not my mistress. I have never thought of you in that manner."

"You don't have to think of someone like that to treat them that way." She flattened her hands against his chest, but didn't attempt to push him away. "You don't have to think of them at all. I get it. I'm neither glamorous nor pedigreed, but, Bastian, I'm so tired of spending every single holiday alone because you have to make an appearance. I'm tired of not being able to tell my family about you, or my friends. Or having to endure one more set up because I'm always partnered with the single guy who spends an evening trying to impress me. I can't tell them I'm not interested or to leave me alone because I'm involved. Why? Because then people will ask questions and I can't answer them."

"Why the hell not?" The last tenuous grasp he held on his temper frayed and snapped. Just how many times was she partnered with other men? And why was this the first time he was hearing of it? "Why not tell them you're involved with someone?"

"Because then they'll ask me who, and what can I say?" she fired back.

"I don't know, Meredith, what do you want to say?" He zeroed in on her expression, the high color in her cheeks, the way her teeth kept gnashing at her lower lip. Twice in the length of their relationship he'd seen her truly angry and never before at him. However, he'd done nothing to deserve her level of ire.

She snorted and rolled her eyes. "Oh, sure, my boyfriend is Sebastian Dagmar. You know, the prince? The one dating a new model every week? It's all a front, he's really with me. You see, he made it very clear from the get-go we should be circumspect. He said we have to keep it quiet or risk having everything about our lives splashed all over the tabloids."

"I never asked you to keep me a secret from your family." He wanted to shake her and the moment the urge gripped him, he released her to back away a pace. A movement caught his eye. O'Connor left his position on the garden's edge and headed in their direction.

As if noticing him was all it took, Vidal appeared in the periphery to intercept the other man.

"Really? And you didn't keep me a secret from yours?" Meredith's accusation jerked his attention back to her. Vidal would deal with O'Connor, but, if the man persisted, then Sebastian would give into his urge to hit something—*him*.

"I didn't tell Armand about you, nor George. One had the power to forbid me from seeing you, the other is an idiot at times, not to mention too young to understand the risk." He blew out a breath and walked three steps toward the bougainvillea they'd imported. "I told you what would happen if we went public," he said quietly. "Because I wanted you to understand how your life might change, and I wouldn't do anything without your consent. I wouldn't take the choice from you."

"I never had a choice—"

"Yes," he grated out the words. "You did. You have always had a choice, but my life isn't simple or uncomplicated. The threats we face are real, the invasion of privacy is real, and the need to protect what is ours—mine—is very real." How could she think she was his mistress? So far, she'd thrown his appearances into his face twice. Cold dread pitted in his stomach. "Meredith?"

"What?" Frustrated exhaustion hung off the word.

Turning, he eyed her. She looked every bit as upset as he felt. "The women—the ones in the articles and the news stories? Do you think they were all my lovers?"

She stiffened, her chin came up, but her lower lip trembled and betrayed her. The ground beneath his feet sheared away. She thought so little of him, of who they were together, she didn't believe he'd been faithful. The roaring in his ears returned and he swallowed his next words because he wouldn't ask the obvious question. *Had she been faithful to him?*

O'Connor's interest and overstepping behavior made a sick sort of sense. He wanted to kill the man.

"Bastian..." She took a step toward him, but he held up his hand and backed away. He didn't trust himself to touch her or be touched by her. His control shredded utterly, to be replaced by a fury so primitive it defied description. "I—I never wanted to think it."

"But you did. And you do." The corner of his mouth twisted up. How cruel was life? In protecting the one person who meant everything to him, he'd convinced her he thought so little of her, thereby making her believe him to be a ruthless bastard. The damn roaring invaded his thoughts and he turned. It wasn't just in his head. He heard the sound of rotors.

"Your Highness!" The shout came from behind him as a helicopter surged overhead. Light glinted off metal. Spinning, Bastian hurtled himself at Meredith, tackling her to the ground as explosions of rock and earth blew up around them.

~

MEREDITH

Chaos erupted and the cacophony deafened her. Sebastian slammed into her and the air whooshed out of her lungs. He pressed her into the dirt, his whole body covering hers. Someone shouted then a half-dozen men closed around them. Bastian was peeled away and hands seized her then suddenly she raced toward the house, yet her feet never touched the ground.

Ears ringing, she stumbled when she landed inside a windowless room. Sebastian pulled her against him, his arms like steel bands. Glancing up, she could see his mouth moving, but the words were almost indistinct. He put his hand on her cheek, studying her eyes.

"I can't—" God, even her voice sounded odd, muffled. "Can't—understand you at the moment."

He nodded once then began running his hands over her hair, down her face. When he continued to her shoulders, arms, and chest, she realized, rather belatedly, he verified she wasn't injured.

"I'm okay," she told him and wished like hell the buzzing ring in her ears would stop. Sebastian continued, undeterred, and only when he was satisfied she wasn't injured did he drag her close again. "I'm okay. Are you?" When she would have checked him with the same thoroughness, he refused to let her go. Instead, he carried her to a low sofa, then sat, holding her in his lap.

His heart raced like a freight train, pounding

as though it planned to beat its way out of his chest. Studying the line of his profile, she found his gaze fixed on the door, jaw clenched. Bit by bit, the pieces of the past few minutes began to fit together.

"Someone shot at us—at you." She didn't even realize she'd said it out loud until Bastian's gaze pinned hers. His cool remoteness melted away. The muscles in his arms tensed and she realized she was shaking. The trembling seized her from head to toe and tears splashed down her cheeks. *They'd shot at Bastian.* Right in front of her, from a helicopter. They would never have had a chance at the shot if she stayed inside.

He crushed her to him and she held on. "I'm sorry. Oh my God, I'm sorry—" She could have gotten him killed. With one hand buried in her hair, and another pressed against her back, his touch soothed her, but couldn't ease the violent shaking.

Fisting his shirt, she buried her face against his neck. The warm masculine scent of him reminded her just how close she'd come to losing him. Again. Before—when he'd been hurt—he'd been so far away and she'd been so damned help-less to do anything for him. Her helplessness eventually turned to anger. *Today? Today I was right there and utterly useless.*

Bit-by-bit, the humming in her ears dulled and the sound of Bastian's ragged breaths punched through her, accompanied by the sweetest sound of his calming words. "We're all right, Meredith. We're secure for now. It's all right." She didn't know how long he'd recited the refrain, but it worked to unlock the cramps in her shoulders and her neck.

"They tried to kill you," she whispered, horrified.

"I know. It's all right. We're all right."

"No, it's not." When she leaned away again, he loosened his hold, but only just barely. "Sebastian, they were *shooting* at you."

He regarded her gravely. "I know, darling. They weren't only shooting at me. What happened today, I never wanted to happen while you were with me."

"How often does it happen?" How could she be completely clueless about it? Sure, he had security, bodyguards, drivers, and rules. He'd always employed a lot of security, but she'd never grasped the reality of it.

With a sigh, he stroked her cheek. "More often than I care to admit. We often downplay it and, if we can, we avoid it being reported at all."

"But, why?" One plus one equaled a big bloody mess, and the math didn't compute.

"Most of the time, attacks are the work of the mentally ill or the politically motivated. Advertising what happened due to someone who is emotionally or mentally unbalanced does no favors for anyone and the politically motivated want the attention, so we deny them the satisfaction. It dilutes the possibility of copycats." The gentle rub of his thumb along her jaw helped unlock another layer of tension, but her stomach twisted with worry.

"Your stabbing wasn't the only attempt on your life." It wasn't a question.

He looked almost apologetic. "No."

She still tried to sort through information when the tumble of locks sounded. Sebastian lifted her up, away, and rose to stand between her and the door so swiftly she barely had time to process his motion. His white shirt did little to disguise the coiled line of his muscles or the level of threat emanating from him.

This wasn't her playful lover, but someone far more dangerous and powerful. A light flashed from red to green on a panel next to the door then it opened. Vidal entered and closed the door behind him. "Your Highness, do either of you require the doctor?"

"Send for him. Meredith should be examined." Sebastian's tone was grim.

"I'm fine," she began to protest, but Sebastian hushed her with a single look.

"You're in shock." He returned to the sofa and slid his hand along her nape. Yes, her heart was racing and she was still panting, but she didn't think she was so bad, was she? Holding up her hand, she stared at the violent trembling seizing her fingers.

Okay, maybe she was.

Vidal pressed two fingers to his earpiece. "The physician is on the yacht. We can take you both there immediately. We've already called for our helicopter."

"Kate flew out first thing this morning. Is she secure?" The mention of the other woman jolted

Meredith and she gripped Sebastian's wrist, holding on for dear life.

"Yes, sir. Miss Braddock is fine. We sustained a couple of injuries and we've notified Greek authorities about the damaged craft. It was smoking when it flew away." Vidal paused and Meredith glanced up to see the censure on Bastian's face a moment before the bodyguard switched to another language.

"Who was hurt?" Meredith wanted to know. Sebastian might have been the target, but there were other people out there—bodyguards and maybe some of the house staff. She'd been too busy arguing to pay attention.

Instead of answering her immediately, Sebastian continued to massage the back of her neck and looked at Vidal. "How long?"

"Ten minutes. I want you both in vests. We'll handle everything else." The man nodded and let himself back out, the light flashing back to red when the door sealed. It was a panic room. The belated realization seemed to come from some distant part of her mind which persisted in trying to sort through the data.

Sitting back down, Bastian pulled her into his lap once more. "Meredith, I need you to focus on me."

"I am." Why did he keep acting like she wasn't? She shifted in his grip and faced him. He was so beautiful, dark and haunted. She'd been so angry with him and now all she wanted to do was hold him and make sure he was all right.

"Your breathing is still off." He frowned.

"Concentrate, slow breaths. In for a count of four and then out for a count of four."

Of course, she could count to four. She tried to obey, but the air seemed to back up in lungs, and she let it out with a whoosh. The quivering sensation was everywhere and icy heat slid over her skin. "You're scaring me. What happened? Who was hurt?"

"O'Connor was hit in the shoulder. He has lost a lot of blood, but two of my men are field medics—Meredith, breathe." The last two came out on a whip of command and she sucked in a noisy gasp and then another under his implacable stare. He exhaled slowly with a nod and continued to rub her back. "They've stopped the bleeding, but he will be on the transport. We have a physician and a fully appointed medical bay on the yacht. He will be all right."

The roaring was back in her ears again. "I have to see him—" *This is my fault.* He was hurt because of her. She'd chosen to go outside. If not for her, none of it would have happened.

"You will, you will." Sebastian didn't let her go. "In a few minutes, they'll bring us bulletproof vests. You will put it on." His tone brooked no arguments. "We'll leave as soon as the helicopter lands. They're securing the landing pad right now."

She clutched onto the control in his words. "Should we leave? I mean if they sent a helicopter before...?"

"This is a stationary target and they've never

come at us here before, but things are changing and changing swiftly. The yacht is mobile and easier to secure. We'll also be able to see anything coming at us." He sounded so matter-of-fact and calm.

"I'm sorry I'm not handling this well." She wanted to do better. "I've never—no one's ever shot at me before and why? Why would they? It's like something out of a movie." A bad movie, a terrible thing, and Bastian? He'd taken her all the way to the ground. He'd covered her so they wouldn't hurt *her*. Flashes of ice and flame consumed her.

"Meredith." The command in his voice snapped through her again and she blinked, bringing his face back to into focus. "Breathe."

Aggravation at her weakness flared. She was a wreck while he was a rock. "How can you be so calm?"

"I am not calm," he said in oblique fashion, but the door locks tumbled again and once more Sebastian rose. Instead of setting her on the sofa, he put her on her feet. He stayed between her and the door.

Vidal entered and passed over a vest. Bastian took care to help her into the oppressive item. It weighed more than she expected, but he made sure it was secure before sliding on his and covering it with a jacket.

"ETA?" Sebastian asked.

"We're ready now. The Grand Duke was notified and has handled security arrangements for the rest of the family. They are all secure. The yacht is holding a stationary course and we'll confirm once we're in the air."

Sebastian pressed a hand to her face. "Stay with security..."

"What? Where are you going?" She hated the needy sound invading her voice.

"Shh." He pressed a kiss to her forehead. "I will be with you, but we're going in separate cars with separate details. Vidal will be in charge of yours."

Which was apparently news to the other man. Shock rippled Vidal's normally placid expression, but he seemed to recover quickly.

"You *will* listen to him, and do exactly as he tells you to do. As soon as we're onboard the helicopter, we'll be together again." He dragged her close and kissed her hard enough to steal her breath then he was gone. She was shuffled into the center of a half dozen very large men, but her heart was in her throat because she could think of only one reason he wouldn't ride in the same car with her.

It still wasn't safe.

CHAPTER 8
SEBASTIAN

S ebastian's laser focus remained on the car traveling behind him—or, better yet, the car beyond. They'd left the main house in a caravan of vehicles, too many to allow for chance. Vidal rode with Meredith, but she'd still been glassy-eyed and her shallow panting weighed on his mind. Shock wasn't pretty and she'd suffered a tremendous one.

"We're almost there, sir. So far we have an all clear. Greek authorities are sending investigators and have requested permission to access the house." The bodyguard in the front seat was on permanent assignment to St. Christos, one he'd accepted because Armand arranged for his family to live there as well. *Hans—his name is Hans.*

"Within reason. The assault didn't take place within the house." The destruction to the garden was considerable. His mother would be heartbroken if she saw photographs—no, Armand wouldn't allow it.

"Understood, Your Highness." Sometimes, his

title had benefits. He didn't feel like explaining himself and, thankfully, the men didn't question his orders. Cooperation in security went both ways, so he let them do their jobs.

"Status on Miss Blake?" It was the second time he'd asked on the short drive and he waited for Hans to contact the other vehicle.

"Shaken, Your Highness. Vidal says she is maintaining a brave front."

Which meant she was still awake. He took it as a good sign. They'd already told him the extent of O'Connor's injuries. He'd been wounded in service to the family, and they would take care of him.

But Meredith was about to have another ugly shock and one he wished he could spare her. His right eye pulsed, and he concentrated on the path ahead. The helicopter waited for them, the men surrounding it not just bodyguards. Retired military, they were armed to the teeth. Another part of his life he wanted to spare Meredith from—the darker, unkind reality of a life lived under siege.

As soon as the car halted, the men created a physical barricade. Sebastian slid into the turtle formed by the men. A similar maneuver would shield Meredith, but he had to wait until he was inside the helicopter to see her. He took her hands and tugged her into the seat next to him. They were airborne before he'd finished buckling her in the seat.

Her sharp gasp told him she'd seen O'Connor strapped to a gurney and secured along the opposite wall with one of the medics attending him.

Of the guards on the island, only Vidal and one other, Beaumont, joined them for the ride. Their pilot was also retired military—British Armed Forces, and a skilled fighter pilot.

Hopefully, they would not need to call upon his particular talent set. Catching Meredith's icy hands in his, he rubbed them slowly. "O'Connor is unconscious. He's lost a lot of blood, but his respiration and pulse are steady." He glanced at the medic for confirmation. The man nodded his assent.

"But there's so much blood—" Meredith swallowed and Sebastian looked at O'Connor. He'd taken two bullets. Unfortunately, the one to his shoulder had punched straight through. They'd at least had the foresight to cover it with a sheet, but it was dark with the seepage of blood.

"Look at me," he told her, needing her focus off the injured man because it wasn't helping her. When she turned her glassy eyes at him, he found a small smile. "He will be fine. The injuries look worse than they are."

"It's my fault," she whispered. "If I hadn't gone out there..."

"No." He refused to let her blame herself. "It was not your fault. It is the fault of the men holding the weapons and those that ordered them there."

Tears shimmered in her eyes and he cupped her cheek. So many things they never said to each other and he'd always intended to tell her...when the time was right. He'd never imagined that their affair would bloom so beautifully or with such depth. Nor did he predict she would read into his desire to protect and shelter her from the ugliness filling the moat around his life as shame. Worse, she thought he only had one use for her.

Anger burned in his gut. That she thought so little of him—of herself—infuriated him. But this wasn't the time to redress their egregious misunderstanding.

"You should have the freedom to go where you want, when you want," he told her, and he meant it. "That is who you are..." His woman possessed dreams, goals, and a desire to pursue them. How the hell could she accomplish them locked in the gilded cage of a life with him?

The flight was one of the longest of his life, but he kept trying to warm her hands and distract her. When she finally leaned her head against his shoulder, he rested his cheek against her hair. The yacht was already en route towards the islands. He'd kept it nearby so he could sweep her off for a romantic impulse.

The yacht's personnel, as with the island staff, were all military. Also, constant roaming made it much harder to pinpoint. They rarely traveled the same routes and they avoided major ports. As soon as they touched down on the yacht's landing pad, Sebastian picked Meredith up and took her below decks. The physician was there to meet O'Connor, and they swept him toward the medical bay while Sebastian carried Meredith to his suite.

While the yacht technically belonged to the whole family, it was his home away from home.

Sebastian lived onboard more often than not. For the most part, he used it to escape the burdens of public life, and it was where he'd first realized how much he loved the woman in his arms.

She roused when he set her down on the bed, but a nurse followed him and Sebastian backed off to let the woman check her vitals. Vidal knocked on the open door.

"His Highness is waiting for your call." The unsubtle reminder that Armand wanted him in contact the moment he was aboard aggravated him.

The nurse glanced toward him. "Her pulse is improved, Your Highness. Doctor Kiriakis will be with her shortly, but I can stay with her until he arrives."

Sebastian focused on Meredith. "Will you be all right for a few minutes? I need to contact my brother."

The watery smile she gave him didn't do much to reassure his concerns, but then she said, "You should call him and let him know you're all right. Do you mind if I take a shower?"

Awkwardness aside, it was the first glimpse of his Meredith since the shooting. "Of course, anything you need." And he said the last to the nurse as much as to Meredith. "I will be back very shortly—"

"Would you check on Terry?" Meredith slid to the edge of the bed and sat. He didn't care for her pallor or shakiness. He cared even less for her request, but clamped down on his jealous response. In all fairness, the man had been injured

141

in their defense and her entreaty wasn't unreasonable or indicative of anything beyond compassion.

"Of course," he said, grateful for the ability to add a smoothness to the response he certainly didn't feel. Unwilling to leave her on such a note, however, he leaned in and brushed his lips to hers. She didn't pull away. Instead, she slid her arms around him. He fought the urge to crush her to him and kick everyone out of the room.

"Will it take long?" Her whisper was so low, he knew it was meant only for him. The need in her voice eased one of the bruises on his heart.

"As swiftly as I can. Shower," he told her gently. "Try to eat something and cooperate with the nurse and the doctor."

She made a face and squinted at him. Her wrinkled nose promised rebellion later, and he accepted the challenge so long as she took care of herself in the meantime. "Yes, sir, but only if you promise to do the same."

He chuckled, and it dislodged another rock from his heart. "As soon as I return." Glancing at Vidal, "Would you have them send in a meal?"

A hint of a smile softened the man's tense face and he inclined his head. "Of course."

Forcing himself to leave Meredith, Sebastian strode out of the cabin and nodded to the man stationed just outside of it. For the time being, they would maintain heightened levels of security. The increased caution meant neither he nor Meredith would be left unattended. Raking his fingers through his hair, he stripped off his shirt as he walked.

"What have we found out so far?" Sebastian asked, as he traded the garment for a clean shirt from his onboard valet.

"The helicopter was abandoned on one of the channel islands, and Greek authorities are on site. They didn't have time for a proper cleaning job, so we're hopeful. The rounds were military grade. We're lucky the winds were higher and the rotors threw off their aim." Vidal followed him into the onboard office. "At this time, we're looking for at least three men. Two witnesses have stated they took a speedboat, most likely headed to one of the larger islands. We've dispatched a small detail to see if they can pick up the trail."

Sebastian shared a look with him. Quietly, oh so quietly, he and Vidal had made a few decisions after the stabbing. Armand insisted on downplaying everything. Instead, he ordered the family to show restraint, but the Belarian general and his people only grew bolder, not less.

"I want one alive. I want to know exactly who is giving the orders." They needed confirmation.

Vidal inclined his head. "Agreed." Instead of leaving Sebastian to his privacy, however, his bodyguard hesitated.

"What?"

"Have you considered sending Miss Blake back to the States?"

"I will not send her away." It was a selfish

choice, but their relationship sat at a precarious point—too damned precarious.

"She will need a new bodyguard, and it cannot be me." Vidal gave him a sanguine look. "My place is with you."

Resting his knuckles against the desk, Sebastian nodded. "Do you have someone in mind?"

"Yes. It will take me about forty-eight hours to get him here. Until then, your detail will handle both of you." Vidal stepped back to let a porter enter and set down a tray with coffee and sandwiches. He waited for the man to finish and leave before continuing. "Until then, eat, discuss what you need to with His Highness, and I will escort you back to the stateroom."

"You're venturing perilously close to giving me orders, Vidal." He gave the other man a wry smile. Few would dare to step over the line with him, but he and Vidal had been together since Sebastian's sixteenth birthday. He was the closest thing to a friend Sebastian allowed himself.

"If one were inclined to instruct a brat prince on his behavior, then perhaps it would be. However, you have been through enough the last few days and you need to settle things with Miss Blake. I can handle security and any other issues..."

"Vidal?" He was going to do something he'd never done.

"Yes, Your Highness?"

Sebastian stared at Vidal's cool features. He'd been privy to their relationship from the beginning. He'd helped to keep Meredith's identity a secret, even from the family. "Can she handle it?"

"It's not my place to answer the question." Vidal's answer was not what Sebastian wanted to hear. "However, if one were inclined to give romantic advice, I would suggest being honest with her. She means far more to you than you've ever told her. You have made many crucial decisions regarding her without consulting her. If she is to be your partner, perhaps you should allow her to be so. Make your call, sir."

It was the closest thing to a stamp of approval he was likely to receive and Vidal was right. He and Meredith had a great many things to discuss. Picking up the handset, he dialed Armand's private number and waited. His brother answered on the first ring.

"Are you safe?" Yes, his autocratic brother cared—oftentimes more than he demonstrated.

"Yes, and unharmed." Save for the ten years he'd lost when he'd realized what was about to happen and how close he'd come to losing Meredith. "We are on board and the captain is taking us out to deep water." They would run under a different flag and adjust accordingly for the time being, avoiding any port waters.

"Send Miss Blake home and stay there until I can make other arrangements. We will cancel the Belarian trip and deal with them another way."

It was so like Armand to give him instructions, but the relief in his brother's voice was profound.

"No." Sending her away wasn't open to negotiation. Neither was canceling the visit to Belaria. "We cannot let them drive us underground. I will not stop living my life for them. I already gave up five years under the presumption I needed to."

"Sending her away is a reasonable response—"

"If I were feeling reasonable, I would agree with you. I am not. If I send her away now, I risk losing her entirely."

"You chance getting her killed if you keep her there." He understood the tightness in Armand's voice wasn't anger, but fear. While Sebastian shared the emotion, his worry went deeper.

"She thinks I'm keeping her as a mistress. I cannot let her feel discarded. I can't." Surely his brother wouldn't force him to decide between his family and Meredith, not now. Not after everything. "Do not make me choose, brother."

"Have you told her?" The truth? The whys behind every step—and apparently his missteps? That he loved her above all others?

"No," he admitted. "But I am planning to." As soon as he got off the phone. Meredith Blake was not his mistress and, by God, she would know it.

"Sebastian, be careful." Armand's tone changed. "Once you make this decision, it changes everything for her."

"It's not only mine to make anymore." It hadn't ever truly been, but he'd thought she understood. Only it wasn't the case—the misunderstanding bothered him more and more.

"Be safe. We're going to handle this. You take

care of your lady. I would very much like to meet her."

If only wishing made it so. "Take care of Anna and Alyx. How many papers have the pregnancy?"

"Only the online gossip columns, but it won't be long now." So, the ticking clock on the world's speculation had run out, and they were not fully prepared. The paparazzi were only a piece of the puzzle and more nuisance than anything. When Belaria learned, the royalists would take it to heart. Therein lay the real problem.

"And George?"

"We've already made arrangements and set up a new name for him. He will not enjoy being out of the limelight, but we've impressed it upon him. Mother was entertaining our cousins, and they are all going to take a very long trip to the country house." Armand didn't have to say the very private and secure country house, since Sebastian understood the decision.

"Is that wise?" Sebastian frowned.

"I do not think they are targets. It's the family name they want to wipe out, which means they'll likely focus on the three of us and Anna."

"And Meredith..."

"Yes." Armand agreed, and they were both silent for a long moment. "Sebastian, did you truly think I would order you not to see her?"

"Brother, you were very unhappy for a long time. You saw only political ramifications and the potential fallout. Also, you did not trust women."

Sebastian hadn't enjoyed his brother's estrangement from Anna. He'd been a miserable bastard.

"Perhaps you're right." Armand's admission didn't make Sebastian feel better. "For what it's worth, I advise caution. If she cannot—"

"I know." He didn't want to discuss what it would mean if Meredith rejected his life. It would break him. "Keep me informed, and do not cancel the Belaria trip. Now, more than ever, we need to show them they cannot hunt us to extinction. If we run, brother, we will never stop."

He was damn tired of running. They spoke for a few minutes more. Sebastian drank a cup of the coffee and picked at one of the sandwiches. Once they'd disconnected, he took the time to check on O'Connor's condition. He'd promised her he would, after all.

Leaving his office, he said nothing to Vidal and the nurse excused herself the moment he stepped into his suite. Meredith sat on the bed, a blanket draped over her legs. She'd showered and changed into one of his shirts.

When the others left, he crossed the room and studied her. Some of her color returned, thanks to the shower he supposed, and she didn't look quite so rocky, but he wanted to be sure. "How are you?"

"You were right about the shock. The doctor gave me something to calm my nerves." Her smile was wan, and she fisted the blanket. "I ate some of the soup, but they brought more food. A proper meal because I wanted to eat with you."

148

He nodded slowly. "Good. Are you up to talking or would you prefer to eat and sleep?"

She gave him a long, uncertain look and bit her lower lip. "You're angry with me." It wasn't a question.

"Extremely," he admitted. "But it can wait. You need to rest." Her health came before all else.

"We need to talk," she admitted.

He took the invitation at her word and nodded. "There are three things you need to know. The first is I have had no lover other than you since we met." Even knowing what she thought, the surprise in her eyes hurt, but he stayed his course. "Secondly, the only reason I never told my family about you was because I did not want to Armand to order me to end the relationship. Had he done so, I would have been forced to choose between my duty and my love. My family needed me then and they need me now. I did not want to have to abandon them."

Her eyes filled with tears. While he wished desperately to comfort her, some truths were better harsh.

"Lastly, at no point have I ever considered you my mistress. If anything, you were my lady. One I waited to claim so you could have the life and the future you craved. The life I could not give you. The life I believed, until a few hours ago, you chose for yourself." He exhaled slowly and remained standing, his gaze fixed on her though he longed with every molecule to join her on the bed. He longed to reassure himself in every way how very alive and vital she remained.

But sex, it seemed, complicated their comprehension of each other. He could not let it cloud their judgment or their understanding, not this time.

"I—my future?" She sat forward, her frown intense. "I don't understand. What future did you think I craved that you couldn't give me?"

There was the crux of it—Meredith didn't understand. "Meredith Blake is a doctor of mathematics, a skilled lecturer, and a highly in demand theorist. She's respected in her field and one of the youngest professors to receive tenure. She is amazingly gifted, deeply respected, and—" He recalled Daniel's reaction to her. "—highly prized for her abilities and work. She is, in all things, at the top of her field with a very vibrant future. Did you not say you have received multiple offers? You've published four times in five years, and your work is invaluable. You have provided insights, which have made or broken projects. All of those things were possible because you were not Meredith Dagmar, princess and wife of the second Andraste son. As my wife, you would have led an altogether different life, one you suffered a taste of today."

Her eyes widened, and she sucked in a noisy breath. Sebastian barely smiled because it seemed unlikely she could have manufactured her response, yet...how could she not have realized?

"I had no idea."

"Didn't you?" He canted his head. "You said I kept you a dirty little secret, that you were my mistress. You reconciled yourself to your position in my life." Damn if her words still didn't cut him. "Although at all times you held the power to change it and chose not to."

Anger sparked in her eyes. "How the hell did I have the power when I didn't even know you wanted to marry me?"

"One phone call, Meredith. One call to the press telling them who you were and what we shared..."

"Then they would have been all over me. You warned me during our first weekend together. You told me to only show what we wanted them to see—" She stopped, and her lower lip trembled.

"Exactly." This time he did smile, but it held no happiness for him. "As long as you wished for the life you wanted, I wished for you to have it. I wanted you safe. I wanted you to be able to chase your dreams and did not leash you permanently to my side without hope of privacy. When you stayed quiet, when you chose to keep us a secret, I knew it was what you wanted, too."

"I—" She began then paused. An intense struggle played across her face, and she shuddered. "I thought—I thought we were having fun and fun was what you wanted from me. I loved—"

His heart jerked at her hesitation. "What?" he demanded. "What did you love?"

Soulful brown eyes locked on his. "I loved being with you and, even if all I could have was a piece of your life, I wanted that piece."

"Until you didn't anymore..." He finally gave into the urge to be closer to her. Her shoulders jerked as his words found their mark. "Until, for some reason, out of all the many lovers you believed I dallied with, the last unremarkably ridiculous story of my supposed engagement tipped the scale. Why then? What changed?"

When she didn't answer immediately, the seeds planted over the last few days—based on O'Connor's outright refusal of orders to his belligerence to the open affection between the two—blossomed into cold certainty.

"Or should I ask *who* changed your mind?"

She didn't answer directly, only frowned. "What are you talking about?"

Needing to touch her, he stroked a finger down her cheek. Would he be able to forgive her if she admitted his suspicions were correct? Would it break him if she did? "O'Connor," he supplied. "Is he your lover?"

～

MEREDITH

An academic, raised by academics, Meredith rarely lost her temper. In fact, her parents' one steadfast rule throughout her childhood involved never discussing or debating in anger. If she couldn't be reasonable and rational, then she wasn't welcome at the table. The lesson served her well, until Bastian asked her about Terry.

"He's my *friend* Sebastian. Don't make our argument about Terry."

He curved his fingers against her cheek and ran his knuckles up the line of her jaw. "I'm not making it about him. However, your concern and affection coupled with his actions and attitude... they leave the situation open to interpretation."

Pulling away, Meredith tried to wrestle the flames engulfing her thoughts. "My *concern* and affection, as you call it, are for my *friend*. Maybe you haven't noticed, but I've known Terry nearly as long as I've known you. You hired him six months after we started seeing each other." Despite the shot the doctor gave her earlier, her heart began to pick up from a dull thud to a plodding canter. Scrubbing her hands against her face, she stared up at him. "You did not just say you wanted to marry me buried in a qualified argument regarding my future then ask me if I was sleeping with another man?"

Sliding his hands back into his pockets, he regarded her with a brooding look. "A question you haven't answered directly, and you're not one to play games, so why are you avoiding it?"

Shoving off the bed, she ignored the sway of the boat even as it made her stomach a bit queasy. Sebastian's gaze scorched her as he looked her over from head to toe. His shirt struck her mid-thigh and she'd chosen it—a choice she now questioned—because of all the clothes in his stateroom closet, it held onto some of his scent.

"You shouldn't be up."

"Oh, stuff it, Your Highness." She scowled and

stomped over to the table. And yes, she was stomping. *Marriage.* At no point in five years had he ever brought up marriage. Him throwing it into the middle of the argument knocked her sideways. Then, to add upheaval to topsy-turvy, he wanted to know if she was sleeping with Terry.

"Excuse me?" He was right behind her when she made it to the side table where a porter delivered the trays with soups and sandwiches earlier. Ignoring him she plucked up silver lids to find a selection of fruits and cheeses. She slammed them back down with a somewhat temper appeasing clang.

"You heard me." She bumped into him as the boat did another little roll over some wave. He put his hands on her hips to steady her. Shaking him off, she jerked up the next domed lid only to find tiny crescent cut sandwiches. Clanking it down, she looked under the third.

"For the love of God, do your people not ever serve chocolate? I need liquor or chocolate for this discussion. Since I can't drink thanks to the shot, I want chocolate."

Whirling she faced him and, had her mood been less dark, the utter surprise in his expression might have been comical.

"No, I've never slept with Terry. I've never even considered it. Yes, I've slept with him in my house on more than one occasion. He's held my hand during take offs and landings for the last seventeen trips because planes scare the crap out of me. If you understand the math of velocity, they'd scare the crap out of you, too. He was there when I got the news about your stabbing, and he held me while I cried. He's the only person I know who knows who you are and what you mean to me. He also held his ground and tried to protect me when I decided I couldn't do this anymore."

She took a step toward him and planted a finger in the middle of Sebastian's chest. "It bothers you he's *friendly* with me and he *oversteps*? Guess what? I have to stare at buxom models, practically spilling out of their clothes, hanging all over you, all the time." She punctuated each word with a thrust of her finger against his chest. "So suck it up and get me some chocolate."

It nearly ruined her demand when she weaved her way back to the bed, but she sat with a thump and folded her arms. Sebastian eyed her a long moment before saying in a soft voice edged by concern. "You're afraid of flying?"

Really? She stared at him. *That* was his takeaway? No, she wouldn't answer him. Not while her emotions staged a prison break and rioted through her system. The physician gave her a sedative because she'd experienced a rather rude anxiety attack thirty seconds after Sebastian left the room. Terror from the whole day swamped her. Sebastian lived in a fortress barricaded by armed guards. She'd always known about the potential danger, because his security was rather impossible to miss, but she hadn't understood the ramifications, not truly, until today.

A moment later, she heard him pick up the phone and say, "We need chocolate. Yes, hot chocolate is fine, but...No, just bring all of it. Thank you." He hung up and a couple seconds passed before the bed dipped with his weight. His arm came around her. She stiffened, but he didn't pull her to him so much as drop his chin onto her shoulder and hold her.

Only the hushed sound of his breathing filled the quiet. She could feel the steady thump of his heart where his chest pressed against her back. The rigidity in her spine began to ease because of his nearness. Being surrounded in the rich masculine scent of him further calmed her, but beneath the smell of him, she could detect the barest hint of cordite—gunpowder. He didn't have the time to shower or do much of anything since the island attack, too occupied trying to look after her and Terry.

"I don't want to fight with you," she whispered on a sigh. His arm tightened once, but he said nothing. After a long moment, she frowned. "Bastian?"

"I'm not saying a word until the chocolate gets here," he told her solemnly.

Surprised, Meredith twisted to look at him and, beneath his very serious mask, a glint of humor warmed his eyes. The corner of her mouth started to twitch and, as one, they burst out laughing.

CHAPTER 9
SEBASTIAN

True to his word, Bastian didn't say anything until the chocolate arrived. When it did, he filled two mugs with hot cocoa and set up a tray on the bed. By unspoken agreement, they sat across from each other. The chef sent up a tray of chocolate delicacies from strawberries wrapped in dark and white chocolate to mousse. "You know, a candy bar would have sufficed."

The corner of his mouth curved up. "Don't tell Philippe. He will be disappointed if you don't enjoy these. Desserts are his favorite to prepare, though I admit his talents are wasted on me and my brothers."

"I suppose offending him wouldn't help anyone." Meredith wrinkled her nose, but picked up one of the strawberries.

"No." He sighed and set his mug down on the table next to the bed. The weighted bottoms on the cups and plates kept them steady. It was amazing how comfortable she was with the sway of the yacht. It had taken her several visits to acclimate. "Meredith, are you really afraid of flying?"

She sighed, wishing not for the first time that she hadn't blurted her confession out. "Yes. It makes me nervous. The doctor gave me a prescription, but sometimes I don't have it with me." Like when he would surprise her, sending a car to the school to fetch her with no warning. She'd leave without even a bag to her name and endure the trip. "I got used to it, and you were always waiting for me on the other end of the flight."

"Why didn't you tell me?" He frowned. "I've flown you all over the world."

"I know." Meredith finished the strawberry and reached for one of the glass dishes filled with dark chocolate mousse. Dipping her spoon in, she shrugged. "I wanted to see you and it never seemed important once I was there. I'm not always afraid. You actually make me forget I'm on a plane when you're with me."

His expression softened. "Be that as it may, tell me when something frightens you. I can't fix it if I don't know there is a problem."

"Oh, you mean like me not knowing you wanted to marry me? How was I supposed to know, again?" She pinned him with a look. "Which conversation about that lovely little gem did I miss?"

Bastian leaned his head back and let out a groan. "I've wanted to propose since our first anniversary."

Her spoon halted halfway to her mouth.

They'd been on the yacht during their first anniversary, her very first trip. He surprised her, one of many over the course of their weeklong interlude. She remembered it was the first time Bastian made sure it was only the two of them. Even with the yacht's staff and his regular security, she'd seen very little of anyone besides Bastian. They'd sailed through tropics, swam in crystal clear waters, and just played together. "I don't remember a proposal..." Granted, they drank a *lot* of wine over the duration of the week, but she'd remember regardless, wouldn't she?

Amusement warred with exasperation in his expression. "Do you remember the night we dined on the deck?"

She remembered skinny-dipping afterward, and her face heated. Bastian showed her the glowing plankton and fish. The water had been warm, like silk. Clearing her throat, she nodded and stuffed a spoonful of mousse into her mouth to keep the decadent thoughts to herself.

His smile deepened, revealing his dimple. Everything in her went low and tight. She loved him so much. "I am referring to the dinner, not the beauty afterward."

"Yes." She blushed and dipped her head to let her hair fall over her face. It never failed. He could turn her into a puddle of schoolgirl neuroses and longing with one look. "I remember. We ate something incredibly fancy with four names and seven courses and a bottle of very expensive French wine that you told me a story about."

This time he gave her a true grin. "And they delivered the black velvet box with the dinner."

"Oh, the necklace—" She scooped up more of the chocolate and ate it. Nerves fluttered like mad to race around the core of heat blooming in her belly. "It was far too expensive." So many diamonds—chocolate diamonds, he'd called them. The piece was absolutely exquisite. "It was—it was beautiful." And far too much for her. He'd put it around her neck, insisting she at least try it on and, when she'd seen it there? *Wow.* Her heart had done a little summersault.

"Do you remember what you said?" His gaze locked on her as he picked up one of the thin wafers of chocolate and offered it. Leaning forward, she accepted it and laved her tongue against his skin just to watch the heat scorch across his eyes. Yes, she knew how to get to him, too.

"I said I could never wear it." She'd always regretted reality intruding into their moment. "I was in my first year of tenure, so I really needed to prove myself. Those diamonds were exquisite, but too much." If she'd stopped there, it would have been fine, but she'd said more.

"And?" he prompted.

Meredith sighed. "And I'm not one of those women you drape in diamonds and then escort around like some type of arm ornament." She made a face because, while the words were bad, they really weren't the worst. "Don't get any ideas about me. Do I look like I want to be a princess?" She grimaced and put a hand over her mouth. "Please tell me you weren't planning to propose."

"I would, but it would be a lie." Sebastian tapped her nose lightly. "You had plans, Meredith. Big plans. You spent the next hour telling me how you were going to rock the academic world. You were so alive with it, practically sparkling."

"So you just decided to not ask?" Had they missed their opportunity because of her ambition?

"I decided what I wanted more than anything was you by my side, but I wanted you happy to be there. I wanted to ensure your freedom to chase your dreams. How could I ask you to give up your plans and aspirations with only me as poor recompense?" *The earnest simplicity in his response...*

"Wait a minute, how are you poor recompense?" She straightened and caught his hand when he would have pulled it back. This was important. "If I don't get to call myself nobody, you don't get to call yourself a booby prize."

"My life is dictated by rules, rituals and guards—"

"And death threats." It made her cold just to think about it. "But Bastian, you're wonderful. You see all these beautiful things everywhere you go. I mean you *really* see them. The artists along the Seine, how many did you sponsor? Or the lady with the dolls in Belgium. You paid for her home then gave her a stipend so she would keep making those dolls for children. When the Canadian floods nearly shut down a zoo because the damage was so extensive, I know it was you paid for the repairs. It wasn't your brother, his company, or his title, but you."

"I didn't tell you about the zoo." A frown arrested his features.

"No, but you called me." It was her turn to grin. "I heard elephants in the background. I remember you saying you needed to delay our trip by a day, and I could hear the animals. Still, you wouldn't say why. A couple of weeks later, there was a special on one of the news programs about a secret angel who rescued the whole shebang."

"You assumed it was me?" His neutral tone proved difficult to decipher. Was he surprised she'd noticed? Or worried he failed to hide it as well as he'd believed?

"If you didn't want to tell me, I assumed you must have your reasons." She'd made assumptions, but so had he. Their entire relationship was built on a tower of presumption. Mirth failed her. "Have we screwed this up? Irrevocably?"

"No." She believed the stern conviction in his voice. "I have damaged your trust and given you fair reason to question your faith in me."

His declaration brought her upright. "Bastian—"

He squeezed her hand, tugged her forward, and pressed a firm kiss to her lips. "I don't like to be interrupted."

"I'm aware." She grinned. "I do it because you need to be reminded you aren't the only one in the room."

"Never when you're here. You're the only one

I see," he told her. "But listen to me for now. Please?"

It was the please that did it. He so rarely said the word, and she knew he implied it more often than not, but he was a man raised to give orders, not make requests. "All right, but can we move the tray? If I dive face first into all this chocolate, I'm going to be bouncing off the walls." Also, she wanted to be closer to him.

After releasing her, he shifted the tray over to the counter housing the other food. When he returned to sit on the bed, she crawled right up next to him and slid her arms around him. Certainly, they had a lot left to talk about and, yes, part of her was still angry. But even when he'd thought she might have taken Terry as a lover, he hadn't pulled away from her. The memory of his constant care and comfort—always—bolstered her courage.

"All right," she told him, after snuggling up to his warmth. "I'm listening."

He chuckled and tangled his fingers in her hair. A light tug tilted her head back to meet his gaze. "I can think of far more pleasant diversions than baring my soul when you're like this."

Good. She'd wanted to remind him as much as herself, but she made a face at him. "No nookie for you, mister. We know exactly how compatible we are there."

"Yes, we do." He cupped her throat and a shiver scissored her resolve. "I know I've damaged your trust in me, and I will do everything to repair it. I have never lied about needing you in my life. Even the small parts we share are so much more preferable to nothing. I will take you however I can have you. I love you, Meredith."

Then he said those magical words aloud. Thank God she'd been sitting, because she wanted to melt into a puddle. "Oh Bastian...I love you, too." She had no idea who reached for who first, but his mouth was on hers, demanding access, and she surrendered to it. He cupped her breast through the shirt, and she went from longing to molten in seconds. Dragging at his lower lip, she pulled back. "No nookie," she reminded him.

"No nookie," he agreed and kissed the pulse point in her throat. Then she was on her back and he continued his sweet torment by trailing his hot kisses down to the opening of her shirt to the top of her breast.

"Bastian," she groaned. He caught her nipple through the shirt and gave it the gentlest of tugs with his teeth.

"This isn't nookie," he told her. "It's my version of chocolate. I find I can't continue anymore of this without some chocolate." He continued his descent, parting the shirt as he went. She laughed.

"Well, in that case..." His mouth closed over her sex through her panties and she forgot to think at all. The hot wet kiss drove her mad. He pulled away only to strip the fabric down her legs before the heavy, hard weight of him returned. The dip and swirl of his tongue sent her pleasure ratcheting up. It was both too much and not enough.

"Do you have any idea how beautiful you are?" he whispered against her thigh before kissing his way back up to her bared breasts. He lingered on first one and then the other.

She wasn't sure how she could answer under the sensual assault. Her breathing grew rapid as he swirled his tongue over one erect nipple in a back and forth motion which sent heat to throb through her lower body. A moment later, he levered himself up and she could only watch in a daze of utter lust as he stripped off his clothes.

The man had the best body, all tense and rippled and thick in the right places. Adding his natural charm to the mix along with the dark crown of his hair and the errant lock that fell into his eyes, he devastated her senses. He didn't give her long to look before he covered her naked body with his and captured her mouth for another long, greedy kiss. His hands seemed to be everywhere, stroking, touching, and teasing. When he cupped her pussy, she cried out against his mouth. He pursued her pleasure with relentless demand.

Some fogged over portion of her mind recognized the claim for what it was—he was staking ownership and demonstrating exactly whom she belonged to and it was magnificent. She never wanted him to stop. His finger slid against her clit, teasing it wickedly, and unleashed a torrent within her. Every circular swipe of his finger against her sensitive flesh pushed her higher and she spiraled on delight. He drove her right up to the edge, and her inner muscles clenched at the first invasion of his finger. He pulled back and then slid in a second with another thrust.

Arching her back, she lifted her hips to meet the sensation. A hot smile curved his lips, and his eyes darkened. He knew exactly what he was doing to her. Then he increased the pressure and every nerve ending her body seemed to light up with the promise of her orgasm. Just when she thought she couldn't take it anymore, he pulled his hand away.

She wanted to cry out from the loss, but then he angled and thrust inside of her and never once took his gaze away. Every stroke of his body sent spasms of pleasure spiraling through her. She couldn't look away, the darkness reflected in his eyes held her captive.

So connected to him, she fought to ride the cresting waves. She felt naked, raw and exposed. She loved him so much and his passion and love reflected in the ferocity of his gaze. When his jaw clenched, she locked her legs around his hips, increasing the angle. She could feel him so deep inside, they would never be apart. The shift of his thrust splintered her focus, and she toppled over the edge. He followed her, his hips pumping as his climax took him.

They tumbled together, and he collapsed against her. He rested his forehead to hers, and never once did he look away. "I love you," he told her, which made her want to fly all over again. "Only ever you."

THE NEXT THREE days passed in a blissful haze. Of course, he'd still had issues to deal with and reports from the Greek authorities to go over. The men in the helicopter remained at-large. According to Sebastian's conference call with his brother, Peterson—the head of Armand's security —and Jonas Quinn, a man with ties to MI-6 and the family's most recent addition to their European security forces, the chances the assailants would be caught dwindled. The yacht remained in deep, international waters and so far no chatter reached the press. The incident on St. Christos was successfully covered up.

Meredith's fury over the burying of the incident lit her up like a fierce flame from within. He delighted in arguing with her, even as he had to disappoint her vision of what should have happened. Publicizing the incident would not only highlight the family's holdings, but also their vulnerability. No one claiming responsibility indicated an utter failure to complete their mission objective—and they didn't want to give away the strategic value, either.

The answer hardly mollified her, but she'd finally accepted his assurance it was for the best. They spoke, at length, about a number of subjects from her fear of flying to her actual dislike of his London townhouse, which startled him. They'd stayed there three times over the past five years, and she insisted it was creepy. Her detailed history of the place shocked him further. Apparently, it had been home to a rather brutal murder in the 1920s, a fact his realtor never disclosed. Then again, perhaps the man simply hadn't known.

Sebastian resolved the issue immediately. He would sell the place or donate it to a family in need and transform it with better memories. She'd gaped at him when he'd made the suggestion then laughed. He could get drunk off her laughter.

O'Connor, thankfully, was already on the road to recovery. Sebastian escorted Meredith down to visit with her bodyguard and, for the first time, he tried to observe their interaction through a lens not discolored by jealousy. Odd for a prince to envy another man anything, least of all the comfort of friendship they found in each other. But he wanted it to be him Meredith turned to, not O'Connor. It was a goal worth aspiring toward.

When the subject turned to other likes and dislikes, she'd pointed to their varied course meals and asked why they couldn't simply have a hamburger or an actual sub sandwich. Not everything needed to be gourmet.

Sebastian mentioned the chef might not be thrilled with such a banal request, and she'd merely given him a look. He should have understood what her expression meant, because an hour later she'd disappeared. He found her in the kitchens, cooking.

He leaned against the counter, watching her browning two meat patties in a pan. Philippe hovered in the background, as did Vidal and Gen-come, Meredith's newly arrived bodyguard. Se-bastian met the dark-skinned Frenchman upon arrival and signed off on Vidal's selection. Claude Gencome offered a varied history as an inspector with the French police—one of the youngest—as well as a decorated if unremarkable military record. What Sebastian approved of was Vidal's endorsement and Gencome's no nonsense atti-tude when he'd been introduced to Meredith.

She'd complained at first, worried about Terry losing his job, but Sebastian pointed out O'Connor needed time to recover and then to re-cuperate. When he was well, they could revisit the arrangement. If Sebastian had his way, Meredith would be a permanent addition to his household by then and O'Connor would be back in Boston.

"You know I could come find you when these are ready," she told him over her shoulder. She'd stolen one of his shirts again, not that he minded. It looked far better on her than him. Though they were in the Mediterranean, the temperatures were chillier, so she wore slacks and a pair of deck shoes. His closet held several items for her to choose from, all of which belonged to her after being left behind or purchased for her other vis-its. He liked seeing her clothes hanging next to his.

"I find watching you cooking fascinating."

She stuck her tongue then grinned. "Boy, do you need to get out more." The casual ease with which she issued her challenges seemed to have also grown in the intervening three days. Meredith teased so rarely, yet she'd relaxed enough to pick on him. He adored it. "Cooking is not something I do very well. Mom could burn water, but I do know how to make burgers and I make a mean meatloaf."

He had no doubts about her skill. "I've never eaten meatloaf."

"No?" She flipped the burgers. "It's a very steadfast meal with corn and mashed potatoes. Yum. I really like it on particularly cold nights. If I can get Philippe to forgive me for bastardizing his kitchen, maybe I can make some for you while we're here."

Before he could answer, the chef straightened. "It would be my great honor to host your meal preparation, ma'am. If you will agree to share with Philippe the recipe so he can prepare it for your future requests?"

Meredith swung her head around to stare at the chef. "Did you really just refer to yourself in the third person?"

The chef nodded once. "The frying of 'burgers' is simply compacting the ground beef and adding some spices, yes? Do you cook it fully or to medium rare?"

"Depends on how you like your burger. I prefer mine to be mostly cooked, so medium to medium well. Sebastian's a rare meat kind of guy, so we're going for medium-rare with his. Do you have ketchup?"

It took all of Sebastian's considerable training not to laugh at the man's expression.

"No, ma'am. I'm sorry, I don't. I will add it to the next shopping list."

"Maybe Bastian won't like it." She glanced back at him. "You've tasted ketchup, right?"

"Oh yes." He reminded her, "When we ate french fries." A midnight snack during a long weekend in Vancouver when he'd surprised her at a conference. It had been dreadful, but he'd buy stock in the red goo if it made her happy.

"Oh, right! French fries—" She looked back at the kitchen. "Do we have potatoes? I can make up some."

It was too much for Philippe. He muttered an imprecation in French and pulled out several from a bin. Instead of giving them to her, he began to clean and peel them before chopping furiously.

Meredith bit her lip and looked away. For an instant, he thought the chef's manner upset her, but then he caught the mischief in her eyes and he wanted to laugh all over again. She'd been tweaking the poor man. He'd have to give him a raise.

When she declared the burgers done, they settled in the dining room to eat—she'd conceded the kitchen back to Philippe. Meredith watched him take his first bite of the monstrosity she'd constructed by adding lettuce, tomatoes, onions and cheese and, though she'd decried the hard rolls Philippe sliced for buns, Sebastian actually liked them.

"Well?" she asked after a protracted silence while he chewed.

"It's excellent." He grinned. "Even more so because you made it for me." It warmed him in a way he couldn't quite express. She'd taken the time to fix him something for no other reason than she'd wanted to share her enjoyment.

She took a bite of her own and laughed around the size of the bite. Her rich brown eyes danced with merriment. "I still can't believe you haven't eaten fast food or burgers or something at some point. Didn't you say Armand loved pizza?"

His brother's love affair with the food had more to do with Anna, Sebastian suspected, but then he'd continued to eat it even in the years they'd been apart. Usually alone or with his friend Richard, always over beer. Another difference, Sebastian supposed.

"Bastian?" Meredith touched his arm, drawing his attention back to her and her question.

"Yes, Armand loves pizza." He captured her hand and kissed it lightly before letting her go back to eating. "It was a habit he developed while away at school. He wanted an all-American, normal experience, so I think he ate quite a bit of the fast food you're referring to."

"But not you?"

"I didn't attend an American university." He shrugged. "I went to Cambridge and our father passed away during my first full semester. I had to leave school for a time, but then returned in the following autumn. With the change, it also heightened my security and notoriety. The days where Armand could disappear among the populace were long gone. Too many in the press wanted to know what we were doing, and who we were seeing. It made everything more difficult."

Meredith sighed. "I'm sorry."

"It was what it was. Interestingly, I didn't fully grasp the burden Armand carried all those years. I was, for all intents and purposes, his heir. Still am. Thus, what was once his security burden became my own." He refilled his wine glass then topped off hers. It amused him that she'd actually chosen one for the meal, but then again she did know his preferences.

"So, you weren't as surrounded before your father passed?"

Pleased with her questions, with the fact she wanted to know, he couldn't help the stirrings of old regrets. Regrets he'd long since thought he'd abandoned. "No, not at all. I had Vidal. He came to work for us just after my sixteenth birthday. I graduated from boarding school, and wanted to take a couple of years off to merely travel. So Vidal and I went backpacking across Europe. Well, sort of." He grinned. "It was a good time. We traveled through small villages and towns. Avoided all of the larger metropolis' and, though he insisted we drive rather than walk or ride motorcycles, it was just the two of us with the occasional downtime in a city for him to have some days off."

"Which also explains why you two are so

close." Understanding kindled in her voice and, though he'd never considered it, he nodded.

"I suppose. It was only a few months. When I decided on Cambridge, I needed to study for the entrance exams and Vidal headed a detail of three. We occupied a building with several flats off campus. It made it easier for them to secure me. After my father passed, well, the detail became eight, which limited my options considerably. I was Armand's heir and, as such, I had to be protected. It was my duty to allow it. Armand bore enough of a burden and a steep learning curve in taking over all of our family's holdings."

Pushing back her plate, she brought her knee up and rested her chin on it as she studied him. It made her look all of twelve, except for her eyes. Those eyes searched his and saw far too much. "You wanted to help him, which is why you studied business and diplomacy."

He nodded once. "I changed my field of study, yes. Our father planned for Armand to come work for him after he finished his university experience. He would have learned the company and our holdings at our father's side. His death changed everything. Armand was barely twenty-two and suddenly he was forced to make a billion dollars' worth of choices. The livelihood of, at the time, some thousand employees depended on his choices. Arguably more, if you consider all the companies we do business with. He needed someone he could talk to and I was the someone."

Armand hadn't liked the idea any more than

Sebastian, but there were any number of nights his brother called as he'd weeded through one report or another and they'd hashed out the decision between them. If nothing else, Sebastian learned to understand the intricacies of negotiation. "His friend, Richard, was invaluable later, after he graduated law school. He went to work for us immediately. During the interim, I did what I could."

She picked up her wine glass and swirled the red slowly. "What did you want to study? Before?"

It was his turn to shift uncomfortably. He focused on the burger, finding it very interesting. But the weight of her gaze pressed down upon him and, after two bites, he couldn't avoid looking at her. "It isn't important."

"Now I really want to know." She set her glass down and leaned forward. "What were you planning on studying?"

"Meredith, the burger is excellent and the fries as well."

"Thank you. Philippe made those, and don't try to change the subject." She tapped her finger on the table. "You do realize your life is public record? I can go look up what you studied at school before—"

"I sincerely doubt they have the information accessible." Or at least he hoped they didn't. He wiped his hands on a napkin and finished the glass of wine.

"Fine, I'll pull strings." Meredith grinned. "You may be connected internationally to all the royal bloodlines, but I've got academic pull."

"You're really not going to let this go." He sighed and, in spite of his wish to the contrary, it warmed something in his chest that she wanted to know.

"Nope." She shook her head. "We've been letting so much go and making so many assumptions. I want to know you, all of the little pieces and the big."

"Very well." He rose and held out his hand. Her immediate acceptance and bounce to her feet gratified him. "If you would come with me, beautiful one?"

A faint pink blush brightened her cheeks. "Hmm, I get all shivery when you talk like that."

"Then I must make a point to do it far more regularly." He kissed her knuckles and led her from the room. Vidal and Gencome followed at a discreet distance. Through the yacht, he escorted her, and then to an observation room kept locked. It was a private room, even the staff remained outside of it. If it needed to be cleaned, they could only enter with one of the select few guards in attendance.

Unlocking the door, he caught Meredith's ripe curiosity and steeled himself for her reaction. "What you want to know is in here," he told her and let her enter ahead of him. He nodded to Vidal and the men took up a position outside the door. Meredith paused in the center of the room and turned in a slow circle. He tried to gauge her reaction to the canvases scattered around the room, of which at least three were of her. Reminded, he glanced to the corner and was relieved—the nude was hidden behind another stack. Perhaps he'd save showing her that particular work for later.

"You paint..." she whispered, a note of awe in her voice. She walked over to one of the landscapes, a piece of a small farmhouse in Burgundy. He hadn't yet managed to capture the boy on the footpath correctly, and the light bothered him. "Oh my God, Sebastian. They're beautiful!"

CHAPTER 10
MEREDITH

An artist. Sebastian was an artist. It was like the interlocking, yet oh so vital, centerpiece she'd been missing of a puzzle. He painted everything—landscapes, people, and scenes from mythology. The emotional depth of the works took her breath away. He stood patiently while she walked from stack to stack and began to page through the canvases. The only tense moment came when she walked toward the corner. His shoulders stiffened and the look of the prince arrested his features, wiping away his expression.

"Did you not want me to look at those?" If it bothered him, she would stop. That he'd shown her at all, it was a gift.

"It's—" He hesitated and touched a hand to her shoulder as he moved past her to the corner she'd been intent on exploring. "I want you to see, yet I'm nervous at the same time."

Because he'd bared his soul to her? Who wouldn't be? She kept the thought to herself, so

179

full of wonder at how he'd kept so much talent locked away from everyone. "I can wait until you're ready."

He paused and glanced over his shoulder, a questioning look in his eyes. "I don't want to keep anymore secrets between us."

"Nor do I, but this...?" She twirled her finger in a circle and let her gaze drift over the beauty he'd created. "This isn't a secret, Sebastian. This is your soul and you have a right to share only when you're ready. Thank you for showing it to me now." She pivoted slowly and mirrored her finger's gesture, until she'd turned all the way around and faced him again. "This explains so much about you. All the places we've gone, why you *see* so much more in those places and people..."

He dropped his chin and the stray lock of hair fell over his forehead. A small smile, one of near boyish pleasure, turned up the corners of his mouth. "You truly like them?"

"I love them. I can't imagine how you've kept it from everyone. If I could do this, I'd want the whole world to see." Then again...she looked from the art to Bastian. "But maybe that is why you don't. Because if they saw it..."

He inclined his head and his smile inched toward sad. "Yes, they would see *me*. This is my passion, what I love to do, and perhaps even whom I could have been if things turned out differently. But it is not who the second Andraste son must be, so I paint. I enjoy it, and now I can enjoy you seeing it." He shifted aside some canvases to reveal a large one nearly six feet in height before pulling away the cover.

"Oh." She felt her eyes go round. It was her, all of her, sprawled against the sheets with her hair splayed on the pillows. Her body flushed pink on the canvas and he'd included such detail, even depicting perspiration slipping down her chest. Meredith's face went hot and she covered her mouth, then gaped at the painting again.

"I painted you from memory." There was just enough of an arch tease in his voice to ease her embarrassment. "It is absolutely one of my favorites. I love how you look after an orgasm, so relaxed and complete."

He sounded so damned smug, she started to giggle. "I think I'm rather glad you don't share this talent with anyone."

"This painting is not for anyone's eyes but mine and now yours, hence the cover."

Meredith couldn't stop staring at it. It was pure eroticism, and it made her look so beautiful. "I am not anywhere near as pretty as that."

"No, you are much more beautiful. I need to practice some more to truly capture you." The sincerity in his eyes silenced her argument.

"How did you keep this a secret from your whole family? Surely someone knew." How could they not? Vidal most certainly knew, but he was a vault. He shared nothing about Sebastian with anyone. The trust Sebastian needed to place in his bodyguard meant the man also kept his secrets. He'd told her the same of Terry and any other bodyguard assigned to her. They were hers to trust and they would never report on her.

"Armand had his own interests, and George?" Sebastian shrugged. "I never know what interests George from moment to moment. Mother knew, and I think she suspects I never gave it up. She encouraged me when I was younger, took me to cities with significant art history, hired tutors who could help me grow and, when I went on my backpacking tour? Well, it wasn't so much a tour of cities as it was me looking for things to paint."

Captivated, she sat down slowly on the only piece of furniture in the room, a long sofa. A throw blanket decorated the back. *Did he fall asleep on it after painting all night?* "Painting is why you love this yacht so much." Oh, Sebastian owned homes around the world, but the yacht was always been his favorite. Many in the press attributed the preference to his partying reputation.

He gave her a sideways grin. "Guilty."

"If I'd been your mother, I would never have let you stop this." Surely the woman knew. Sebastian never sounded like she'd been distant with him or left him to be raised by the staff.

Settling next to her, he stretched out his legs. "I don't think she wanted me to give it up, but like Armand and me, circumstances dictated she support my pursuit of a business degree. Mother would never forbid us pursuing our passions, but she raised us to support our family first." Trailing his fingers along her thigh, he shifted sideways to stare at her. "Will you pose for me?"

"Um, all I have to do is sit still, right?" He'd seen her in every stage of undress, helped her get there more than once. She had no reason to feel shy yet—staring at his work, having the very real evidence of what he saw when he worked—she recognized posing for him would leave her in an oddly vulnerable position.

"Yes, but you don't have to be nude for it. I vote for nude, but we'll only do what you're comfortable with."

"Okay, but not right now." She wagged a finger at him as he sat forward. "I actually want to ask you a question about your mother."

"All right." He canted his head and gave her a searching look. "She knows about you."

The simple revelation floored her. "Really?"

He nodded slowly. "I don't know if you remember, but when I took you to the opera in New York, she was there. She just happened to be in the city. I'm fairly certain she paid off my pilot to let her know the next time I flew you out to meet me." His mouth twisted with a hint of sardonic amusement. "So, once she was there, the first thing she asked was to meet you."

"But you didn't introduce us." The sting of his choice still hurt.

"No, because I didn't want to scare you off." Sebastian slid his hand around her nape and nudged her to face him. "My mother is a princess in every sense of the word. She was born to gentility, and it's ingrained into her bones. Even so, she has absolutely no problems with bending all of her sons to her will. She wanted to meet you because she wanted a chance to interrogate you."

Okay, maybe not meeting her then wasn't such a bad thing. She swallowed. "What did you say to her?"

"I told her you were the love of my life and I wouldn't allow anyone to drive you away. I wanted to introduce you both when you were ready, not a moment before, and, if she loved me, she would give me my wish." It changed everything, the insight he was granting her. "She glanced past me, said you were coming, then kissed my cheek and whispered..." It was his turn to laugh. "She whispered 'she's very beautiful, and your words make her much more so to me. Do not take too much time. I'm not getting any younger and I'd like some grandchildren to spoil.'"

Meredith's heart lodged somewhere in her throat, and she couldn't quite swallow the squeak that escaped.

He kissed her and leaned back with a chuckle. "She will love you, Meredith."

"Bastian, I don't know anything about being royal." He'd been so open with her, he deserved the same treatment in return. "I'll be honest, it's a lot to even consider. Each and every time I thought about wanting to be with you, I couldn't figure out how I could be a princess."

"You merely have to be yourself and everyone else will adapt for you."

No way could it be so simple. "Really? And the rules? The bowing? The address of others? I mean do I call your brother Armand, or do I call him Your Highness? And how do other people address me? It's—there are rules."

Sebastian dragged her over onto his lap. She straddled his thighs and rested her forehead to his.

"Meredith," he told her. "It is a life lived in layers. Those of us at the center, we know our circle is closed and very small. The further out you go, the more restrained you become. It is no different than you are with your students—gracious, always kind yet firm."

She'd have to give up her tenured position. Leaving school wouldn't be so bad. She'd wanted to prove she could do it, and she'd succeeded. But, her doctoral candidates still needed her.

"We don't have to make any decisions right now." He threaded his fingers through her hair and nibbled a kiss to her lower lip. "Not about titles or children—and most certainly not about my mother. I want to focus on you and me for the time being and I am admittedly quite selfish. I want all your attention."

Looping her arms around his neck, she smiled. "We can't put it off forever."

"We're not," he reminded her with another brush of his mouth to hers. "We're learning about each other the way we should have all these years. I want you to know everything, and I want to know everything about you."

"Except for the ketchup because you really hated the ketchup." Amusement bubbled beneath the nerves in her stomach. Her whole life would change. She'd never thought past the immediacy of them until he mentioned his mother's desire for grandchildren. Her children would grow up in the legacy of his family—and maybe people would want to kill them, too. The troubling thought lingered, but then Sebastian kissed her. The long, slow, wet kiss short-circuited the dark cloud gathering in her mind.

"I dislike the ketchup, but I love how it makes you smile," he told her. "Can you forgive me?"

Tumbling with him onto the sofa, she let out a gasping laugh. "Well, we can't all be perfect..." And then she wasn't thinking about ketchup or paintings or much of anything. Just Bastian.

~

SEBASTIAN

The clock on their escape wound perilously tighter with every precious hour he lost to lengthy conference calls with Armand. The escalation of the attack coupled with the rumors of Alyx' pregnancy weren't coincidence, nor was the rampant speculation in the press. The morning's news clippings suggested he was utterly off the market and the stories danced right along the line of the truth—too close to the line.

They had a leak.

So far Meredith's name wasn't involved, but Kate was on her way to Italy to meet them. She would take Meredith back via a private jet registered to Daniel Voldakov rather than the Andraste family. Claude Gencome would travel with Meredith and a full detail was on the ground in Boston. Her home was secured and they were already running the faces on her campus through a contact at the FBI to make sure no surprises awaited her.

"I know you want to announce it," Armand said calmly.

"It will merely paint a target on her. We've waited this long, we can wait a few more months." A piece of his soul died. He didn't look forward to the lengthy separation they'd need to make sure the news didn't break until they were ready. He and Meredith were in a much better place, and yet it felt too fragile.

"You've said she's a reasonable woman. Surely, if you explain why, she will understand."

Perhaps, in another lifetime, yes. He could only hope they'd made enough progress, she'd forgive him. "I will handle it, Armand." It was what he did. "Have you told Alyx whether or not the baby will have a title?" It was after all, at his brother's discretion as it had been at their father's when his sister married a military man— their daughters were all princesses.

"Not yet. They've only just reached the end of the first trimester and Anna told me you don't discuss such things until well after." His brother's voice softened at the mention of his wife. "She also told me not to get any ideas yet."

Sebastian laughed. "You want children." It wasn't even a question.

"I do, but I am a selfish man and Anna will be

a devoted mother. I worry about being jealous of my own children."

It was a sentiment Sebastian could sympathize with. "You mean like Father." Though he'd been a good man, he'd possessed a few flaws, one of which included the need to have their mother's full attention.

"I don't think he meant to be." Armand didn't dispute the charge. "I never quite understood the position he was in until recently." The sigh he released echoed across the secure connection. "Sometimes I wonder how different our lives would have been, had he not died."

Sebastian wondered the same thing every damned day. "We can't change the past."

"No. We can't."

The echo of a half-forgotten conversation in the weeks following their father's death drifted into his recollection. "Do you resent not understanding before you inherited what a burden it would be?"

"I did once, but I don't think anyone—not even Father—could have explained to me what to expect. The responsibility. The need to not fail and the desire—every once in a while—to merely have a *normal* life. But you and I, we know very little about normal." The maudlin conversation must have weighed on his brother because he changed the subject. "I want to meet your Meredith, and I don't want to wait several months to do it. You will bring her to Los Angeles or make arrangements to send her here. We can use Daniel and his company as cover, since they have

188

every reason in the world to talk. It won't make a ripple in the press."

"You're worse than Mother—" A knock at the door had Sebastian looking up. "One moment, Armand. Come in."

Vidal opened the door and Meredith peeked in. She wore a camel-colored pullover sweater— one she'd pilfered from his side of the closet— and slacks. He really did need to take her somewhere warmer so she could wear less—their cabin, for example. "Am I interrupting?" she asked

"Not at all," Armand answered before he could. "Come in, Miss Blake."

Her gaze landed on the phone on Sebastian's desk and then switched to him. The hesitation while she sought his approval rather than just taking his brother at his word gratified him. "Come. He will be cross if you turn him down and he has always been a bit of a poor loser." The comment had a dual effect. Meredith smiled and Armand snorted.

The bodyguard closed the door as Meredith crossed the room and took his hand. Tugging her down to sit on his lap, he smiled at her, and nodded toward the phone. "Meredith, may I have the honor of introducing you to my brother, Armand? Armand, this is my Meredith. Be polite." The last two words were delivered as a tight warning.

His brother didn't miss a beat, though humor infused his words. "It is a pleasure to *meet* you, Meredith, however unusual the venue. You must be a remarkable woman, indeed, as Sebastian has never been so enthusiastic about another."

"Hello." She laughed then mouthed, *this is weird*.

"He tells me you've been teaching. I hope you'll forgive an interfering older brother, but I did some research on you."

Sebastian flexed his grip on her hip, but Meredith raised her eyebrows. "Well, I suppose that's fair. I did some research on you, as well."

"Indeed." For a moment, his brother demonstrated a glimmer of hesitation. "Dare I ask what you discovered?"

"Depends. Did you like what you found out about me?" The corners of her mouth curved. His woman's intelligence was never a question, but if she felt uncertain addressing a member of his family, it didn't show.

"Tell me, you don't gamble at all. Why?"

Sebastian actually started laughing at the question, but Meredith shrugged. "Most games of chance rely on certain percentages and statistics. Cards are pretty boring because the number of possible combinations declines with every play. It's too easy to know when to bet and when not to. I do like slot machines, though, particularly the animated ones." She waited a moment and pressed her cheek to his. "Sebastian, however, loves to gamble though I'm afraid I make it pretty boring for him."

"What about billiards?" Where was Armand going with his line of questioning?

When Meredith cast him a questioning look,

Sebastian shook his head and mouthed *I have no idea.*

"Billiards is simple geometry, so not a challenge." If her reply didn't throw down a gauntlet, Sebastian didn't know what would.

His brother didn't hesitate to scoop it up. "Do me a favor? Keep that bit of information to yourself. When you come to Los Angeles in a few months, I want you to play with Richard."

Meredith blinked. "In a few months?"

"Time to go, Armand." Sebastian reached out and hung up on his brother. Rude, but effective. Meredith shifted in his lap and stared at him.

"What did he mean, a few months?"

Damn his brother, he wanted another couple of days before they broached the topic. "Armand and Anna have invited us to Los Angeles to stay at the tower for a few days. He really does want to meet you."

"All right." She nodded slowly and began to fidget with the collar of his shirt. "I'd very much like to meet them. I take it they're very busy if we have to wait a few months?" The uncertainty in her question crushed him.

"Not exactly. In a few days—two, exactly—I have to head to Eastern Europe. I have a series of appearances scheduled. We'd initially intended to do them in a few weeks, but they've been moved up." *How much to tell her?* He wanted honesty between them, but the trip—this particular trip—was fraught with a danger which would only make her worry.

"Because of the attack on the island?" They

hadn't discussed it since their first night on-board. A series of lines tightened the area between her eyes.

"Yes." He wouldn't lie about it. "We scheduled appearance in Belaria..."

"Wait a minute. Isn't Belaria the country that wants your brother to resume the throne?" The looseness left her posture as she straightened to face him. Thankfully, she didn't try to slide off his lap. The need to touch her was a fierce ache whenever she was near.

"A faction there does, yes, but—" He held up a finger, asking for her patience before continuing. "It is only a faction. The notoriety we've gained again over the last few months, with Alyx's discovery and Armand and Anna's wedding, has kept us in the forefront of the people's minds. Other factions in Belaria do not want us to return at all. To be fair, Armand has no intentions of honoring what the royalists want. So, to curb the rumors, I am going to a series of dinners and personal appearances designed to show our... let's say our dilettante lifestyle and disinterest in relocating to Belaria permanently."

"What if those are the same people who've been trying to kill you?" She was not a fool. "Going there is insane. You'd be walking into the lion's den."

"In a manner of speaking, yes." He needed to downplay the possibilities immediately. "But it's absolutely no different than any other event I've done. We go with the support of our allies in the British, Canadian and Norwegian governments.

They are all sending delegations, and I am attending as their guest."

"*Why?*" Horror stamped across her face. "So they can have an easier time of killing you?"

"No." He smiled, wanting to ease her fear. "Because they need to know we're not afraid. No matter what their course of action, our family perseveres. We do not want the throne, we do not want to be figureheads for a royalist party, but we will not bow to suppression, nor will we allow a dictator to use fear to intimidate us."

"Then I'm going with you."

"Absolutely not. Right now, the world views you as only a professor, and you have no firm ties to our family. The news of Alyx's pregnancy is out and the speculation about Anna and Armand will begin in earnest. For the next few months, it's crucial we present an enduring front and no other disruptions. That means I have to be free to be the face the world sees—"

"That makes no damn sense." She jerked back to her feet. He followed her as she paced across his office. "I thought we planned to get engaged. Weren't we discussing an engagement over the last few days? Why can't I go with you?"

Because it isn't safe. He exhaled a breath, knowing bloody well the argument wouldn't work. "Because I don't want you there. This isn't open for negotiation. We'll be arriving in an Italian port in the morning. Kate will meet you at the dock. She and Gencome will see you back to the States. A security team is already in place. We'll make an announcement in a few months. Until then, we'll take all due pre-cautions."

Mutiny flared in her eyes. "Oh, we will, will we? Made all these plans, have you?"

"Yes, Meredith. I've been working on this since before your phone call. The family has to see this through—"

"Wait a minute." She backed up a step. "So, the trick Meredith into coming to see you, the soul-searching, and the arguments and the difficult truths—you even told me you loved me and wanted to marry me—but the whole time, you've known you were going to do this?"

"Yes, and I'm sorry if it disappoints you. By now, you have to know I don't have the luxury of putting my life on hold for anyone. I've delayed everything as long as I could until we could reach some kind of accord between us." The words came out harsher than he intended, but the censure in her eyes stung. He'd all but bent over backwards for her. Why couldn't she meet him halfway? "Meredith, I understand this is difficult. If we had a more equitable solution, we would employ it. The best thing for everyone is for you to go home. I will call you every night and, in a few weeks at most, we will be together again. When we are free to announce it, we never have to be apart again."

"Just like old times." There was something brittle in her statement. He stepped toward her and she retreated, one hand held up to ward him off. "I get it. I need to go home. You've decided and you've made all the arrangements. Do me a favor? Why don't you have your secretary send me a calendar so I know when I'm allowed to care again? You know, since you've made all the decisions already. I certainly wouldn't want to mess up your plans."

She whirled and stomped out.

"Meredith," he called, exasperated. *Dammit.* He wanted her safe. Why was she being so unreasonable? Gencome slid to the side so he could see her halted in the passageway.

Turning sharply, she faced him. "I'm sorry, didn't you plan to excuse me? I thought you wanted me to go home."

"That is not what I said."

"No, what you said is you don't want me there. What you said is you made all these plans and arrangements. I'm not a chess piece for you to move at your whim. We're either together or we're not. Apparently, we're not because the man I marry doesn't make decisions *for* me. Now, if you'll excuse me, Your Highness? I apparently have a plane to catch, so I'm going to pack." Then she was gone, striding away with Gencome in attendance.

Sebastian wanted to hit something, and he looked at Vidal. "Not a word."

"I wouldn't dream of it, sir."

CHAPTER II

MEREDITH

I n their stateroom, Meredith stared at the clothes in the closet and realized she didn't have her bag. Hell, she didn't even have her purse. All of it was back on the island, along with her passport, wallet, keys, everything. Perching on the edge of the bed, she drummed her fingers restlessly against her leg and then bounced up to walk again.

How could he just make unilateral decision? Risk his life? Did he expect her to simply nod her head? Pacing back and forth, she glared at the door and then dragged her fingers through her hair. Her emotions waxed and waned between fury at his highhandedness and terror at the idea of him putting himself out there.

From one end of the room to the other she went. It made her so mad she wanted to scream or throw something. Spinning around, she stalked to the door and opened it. Gencome glanced at her, and she gave him a tight smile.

"I'm going to the medical bay. Are you planning on stopping me?"

The Frenchman raised his eyebrows. "No, ma'am. My orders are only to keep you safe."

"Excellent." She closed the door behind her and headed down the passageway. She found Terry half-asleep, face gray with fatigue, but looking better than he did the first day she'd visited him. The nurse stepped out when Meredith took her place next to the bed and Gencome waited outside the door to give her a tacit amount of privacy.

The wounded man opened his eyes and focused on her. He started to try and sit up and she scowled. "Stay put." What was wrong with men? Did they really think they were invincible? "I just wanted to come and check on you."

"You're upset." He studied her with a small frown.

"I'll get over it." As much as it pained her to admit it, she probably would. What choice did she have? If she wanted Bastian, she would have accept him as he was.

"You don't sound terribly happy about the fact." Terry shifted again. A thick swath of bandages coated his shoulder and stretched across his chest. The bullets, she'd been told, tore through his shoulder and broke his clavicle. It could have been a lot worse, even though it looked less than pleasant at the moment.

Her gut churned. Just a few months before, Bastian was in this room with only his bodyguards and the doctor who treated him. She'd been thousands of miles away and then, like now, Bastian hadn't wanted her there. A headache pulsed behind her eye.

Pushing aside the lingering fear, she leaned forward and put her hand on Terry's. "Are we friends?"

"After a fashion. What's wrong?"

"If I ask you something, can you promise me confidence? I mean, you told me once I could say anything to you and no matter what I said, you wouldn't share. That's kind of like being a friend, right? Because, right now, I could use a friend." She really hoped she knew what she was doing, but she was so confused. *Is there a right decision?*

"Meredith, yes, I'm your friend, but it's secondary to being your bodyguard. In either capacity, I wouldn't break your trust. What's wrong?" Despite sounding weak, Terry gave her a firm look. "Tell me."

She opened her mouth then closed it again. The words she wanted to vent wouldn't be easily said, and it felt like a betrayal to confide in Terry. Though he'd calmed since he'd asked her if she was sleeping with him, her fondness for the bodyguard made Sebastian uncomfortable. Rather than complaining, she summoned a smile. "It's nothing, really. I'm leaving tomorrow to go home. I don't think you're well enough to travel with me."

Terry frowned. "Do you have someone going with you?"

"Yes. Sebastian brought in a new bodyguard for me."

"Claude Gencome. He's a good enough man and he came to see me a couple of days ago to ask about your schedule."

A couple of days... Of course, he did. Meredith bit back another sigh. Sebastian planned it all along. "Well, I want you to concentrate on getting better. I'm going to finish packing. Call me when you're able to come home? I'll make you a cake or something." The last sounded lame, but he'd been hurt while looking after her.

He nodded slowly, but despite his weakened state, his gaze remained sharp. "Are you sure you're all right?"

"No." But that was all she planned to share on the subject. "However, I'll figure it out. I have to." Pressing a kiss to his cheek, she straightened. "Rest. Get better. I'll see you later." And then she was on the move again, with Gencome following.

Detouring again, she headed straight for the kitchen. She couldn't leave the yacht in the middle of another disagreement with Sebastian. No, she didn't like what he was planning and, yes, she'd strenuously objected to being dictated to, but walking away mad wasn't the solution either. Philippe proved amenable to her request and promised to have the dinner set up exactly to her specifications.

Back in the stateroom, she took a shower and after, she dried her hair and returned to the closet to pilfer one of Sebastian's shirts. Maybe she could pack a few to take with her. She'd just finished buttoning it when a knock sounded. Snagging a robe, she pulled it on and answered the door. It wasn't the porter with the meal she'd ordered, but Gencome.

"This came for you, ma'am." He handed her a note and the sound of rotors echoed from overhead. Nodding to him, she withdrew into the room and unfolded the slip of paper.

> Meredith,
> I don't want to fight with you. I know you're upset, and I wish I could say the magical words to ease your concern. Unfortunately, I simply don't have them. We've been forced to escalate the timetable again and, in this, I have no flexibility. I'm leaving for Belaria tonight. Gencome will escort you from the ship tomorrow in Italy. Kate will have your things, including your passport. I will call you as soon as I can.
>   All my love,
>   Sebastian

She stared at the note and, even as the content sank in, she realized the sound of the rotors retreated. He'd left.

Just like that, he was gone. Pacing slowly across the room, she sat down on the edge of the bed. She'd crumpled the note in her hand and she unfolded it carefully and reread it. He didn't want to fight with her, so he'd simply left. He promised to call her, but she didn't have her cell phone anymore.

How could he simply leave?

Because I would have objected...and I walked out angry again. Maybe he'd done the right thing. She wanted the man so much it hurt, but God help her, she didn't know if she wanted his life.

~

BY THE TIME she boarded the plane in Ravello, Meredith was a bundle of nerves. As expected, Kate Braddock waited for her onboard with all of her papers. Gencome proved to be a capable companion, but the Frenchman said very little and his watchfulness only increased her tension. She'd received no phone call from Sebastian, but maybe he was still en route in Belaria. It wasn't as though he'd told her how he planned to travel or mentioned his expected arrival time.

It made her sick to her stomach with worry, and she was quiet when she settled into the seat across from Kate. After buckling in, she stared out the window. Had it been merely a week since she'd sat in the same seat? Her entire world shifted in the space of seven days.

All around her, staff prepared the private plane for takeoff and she sighed.

"You look tired," Kate said into the quiet, reminding Meredith of her presence. Where on the first flight Terry sat next to her, Gencome chose another set of seats closer to the main door which allowed her a modicum of privacy.

"Then I look how I feel." She tried for a smile, but gave up when even her poor attempt seemed more trouble than it was worth. "Thank you for bringing my things."

"No problem." The other woman settled back and crossed one leg over the other. "It gets easier."

"What does?"

"The lifestyle of being royal and under siege." A faint smile curved the other woman's lips, but Meredith couldn't tell if she was serious or not based on her dry tone.

"I thought you were engaged to an attorney." Meredith wasn't sure if the same rules applied.

"I am and he spends a lot of time with the family." When she didn't offer further details, Meredith assumed she was done. The jets outside began to power up and the plane began to taxi forward. "But the key to surviving all the nonsense is to focus on what's important."

Digging her fingers into the armrests, Meredith tried to ignore the churning in her gut as the plane began to hurtle down the runway. "You're being subtle on purpose and I appreciate the effort, but my heart isn't in this particular game at the moment."

"I'm not playing a game. Being royal kind of sucks. Don't get me wrong, it has perks, too. It's definitely a trade-off." Kate shrugged. "Of course, I don't understand you and Sebastian."

"What do you mean?" She blew out a breath

and studied her companion, but Kate's expression bordered on neutral.

"It means exactly what I said. I don't understand you. The two of you were in a relationship for five years. One day, you decided it was over and pretty much gave up. When you told him it's over, he moved heaven and earth to get you both in the same place. I get it didn't go as well as you might have hoped and bullets are not a romantic enhancement, but I was under the impression you two worked things out. Instead, when I talked to him, he sounded dead inside. Now, you look like someone kicked your dog."

The plane leveled and Meredith's stomach lodged somewhere near her feet. "He left without saying goodbye after we fought because he'd made decisions without including me." She disliked everything about the situation.

Kate nodded as if her answer made perfect sense. "Okay."

Her simple response gave Meredith pause. "Okay?"

"Yeah, okay. At least it explains why you look like someone kicked your dog." A light flashed overhead. Kate pulled her cellphone out of her pocket and checked the screen.

"I'm glad I enlightened you." Fresh irritation rasped her already bad mood.

The other woman didn't look up from the cell phone. "Don't snap at me. I didn't let him do it."

"I hardly think I did, either. You participated in the charade to get me to the island in the first place, so obviously you know more about the whole situation than I have been advised. Do me a favor? Either fill me in or leave me alone."

Setting the phone down on her thigh, Kate pinned her with a stare. "You know for someone who is arguably a genius—and yes, I did look at your background check and your record—you're really dumb."

Meredith felt her jaw go slack. The statement, delivered in calm assessment, lacked the sting of insult, yet delivered a more than solid whack to her pride.

"Seriously, you see a man for five years, let him set all the terms and you know he's been raised to be in charge. He lives in a world where decisions come down like they are at the right hand of God, yet you're shocked when he doesn't involve you?" Kate's brows inched upwards. "Word to the wise? You want to be involved, you involve yourself."

"You make it sound so easy." Meredith spread her hands and leaned forward.

"If it were easy, it probably wouldn't be worth it. I like this family. They're arrogant, and they're more than a little entitled at times, but they're good people. So, decide if you want to be with him or not. Decide who you want to be when you're at his side because, if you don't, this life will crush you like a bug then you won't be good for anyone, least of all him." If the first wasn't enough, she wasn't finished. "He wants to protect you more than he does his own life. He was the target on the island, yet he covered *you*. He keeps the press out of your life and very focused on him, but when you stood up to him, what happened?"

Who the hell was this woman to judge? Meredith's spine stiffened and she lifted her chin. "He tricked me into meeting him, a brilliant move on his part." One she could applaud for tackling game theory when her response was the most uncertain variable he faced and he'd done it. His actions were beautifully romantic. "I love him. I have decided where I want to be and maybe I won't be any good at it, but I assure you, I can learn anything and I will learn how to do this. This trip he's on? It's dangerous, but he refused to let me go with him."

"Men. Brilliantly possessive, incredibly protective, and wildly hardheaded. And you let him leave?"

"I could hardly stop him." What did Kate want her to do?

"All right, I'll grant you that. Let me ask you this, what are you doing on this plane?"

"I'm flying home."

"Why?"

"Because—"Meredith stopped. Because Sebastian made the arrangements and told her she was going home. Because Sebastian wanted her somewhere safe and far away from him while he risked his life. Because—

"And now she's thinking again." Kate picked up her phone.

Every decision he'd made with regard to their relationship was driven by the need to protect her and... *to help me achieve my dreams. Isn't that*

*what he said? I wanted to be a tenured professor. I
wanted to be published. I wanted to write my own
ticket for the types of problems I wanted to solve...and
I have all of those things.* Her achievements came at
a price—being excluded from Sebastian's life, at
least the public side of it.

She'd never questioned his devotion to his
family, but even with them, he'd buried his own
dreams—his paintings—so he could help his
brother. The trip to Belaria, literally walking into
the lion's den, he did for the rest of his family and
for her. He put everyone else before himself. *Who
put Sebastian first?*

"I don't suppose I can change the course on
this flight, can I?" Would the pilot even listen to
her? She and Sebastian weren't even formally
engaged, at least, she didn't think they were.

"Well, it's definitely a possibility, but I didn't
tell you all of this so you'd rush to be at his side.
He wasn't wrong when he said this trip is dangerous." Was the other woman reconsidering her
suggestion? *Too bad.*

"I should probably talk to Armand..." Hopefully he wouldn't mind her calling him by his
given name. "I don't suppose you have his
number?"

After unbuckling her seatbelt, Kate rose and
held out the cell phone. "Sebastian asked me to
bring this for you. It has direct contact numbers
for everyone in the family, including my fiancé.
Before you call His Highness, I'd suggest Mr.
Voldakov as this is his plane."

Meredith stared at the phone as though it

might actually bite her and then blinked as the other woman headed down the aisle. "Where are you going?"

"To call Peterson. If you're heading for Belaria, we're going to need boots on the ground." Kate grinned wryly. "Then I have to call Richard, so he doesn't have an aneurism about me going with you."

"Is he going to get mad?" She didn't want to cause problems for Kate Braddock, no matter how beautifully she'd manipulated the argument. Although Meredith noted the manipulation, she'd give credit where credit was due—Kate's actions jarred her out of the pit of self-despair. It was a well-deserved kick in the ass.

"Probably, but like I said, you want to be involved, you involve yourself. Richard loves this family, and so do I. Since I lit the match, I have no problem seeing it through. We're still going to take precautions." Kate glanced over at Claude. "Aren't we, Mr. Gencome?"

"Absolutely, Miss Braddock. I would, however, appreciate it if you two never planned world domination."

"Oh, I don't know." Kate winked at Meredith with a grin. "We'd be great at it." With that, she left Meredith alone to make her final decision. She could choose to call Daniel Voldakov and ask him to change the plane's flight orders. She could head to Belaria and find Sebastian, and then park herself at his side. *But I'm a professor of mathematics, not some action heroine in an Angelina Jolie movie.*

She worked with variables and equations. Everything about the trip was out of her realm of experience. *It's like when you're in classroom. You have to be firm, but compassionate.* Sebastian's words echoed back at her. *We don't want their throne, so we have to prove we don't to them...*

The uncertainty principle inherent in every equation relied on balancing factors. Even a decimal point off could change the whole result. Scrolling through the contact list, Meredith selected Daniel's name and pressed dial. When he answered, she took a deep breath. "Mr. Voldakov —" She paused. They'd corresponded for months and talked on a few occasions. "Daniel? It's Meredith Blake. I need your help to move a decimal."

CHAPTER 12
SEBASTIAN

A headache pulsed behind Sebastian's right eye and fatigue weighed him down like the chains of Marley's ghost, but the Canadian ambassador seemed far from done with his long-winded explanation of how negotiations would proceed. Jacobs, it seemed, was a thorough man. For a split-second, Sebastian's gaze collided with the Kachusov's who served as diplomatic secretary for the Belarian government and host to their back-room talks.

The faint smile accompanied by a roll of eyes united them on this issue. They both wanted the ambassador to be quiet. An illuminating moment considering the window dressing set around the opportunity for a member of the Andraste family to negotiate directly with the Kachusovs. A whisper of fabric behind him and motion warned Sebastian of Vidal's approach. Each representative was allowed one bodyguard or personal aid.

"Please forgive the intrusion, Your Highness, but there's been a development." The man's low-voiced warning was interrupted when the doors to the darkened conference room opened and Sebastian's heart hurtled to his feet.

Meredith stepped inside with Gencome a single pace behind her. Every man at the table rose. If Vidal hadn't tapped his arm, Sebastian would have circled the table to rush Meredith right the hell back out of the room.

The Canadian ambassador turned with a wide smile. "Oh, excellent. I was worried I would have to further bore my audience. Forgive me, gentleman," the ambassador continued. "Please allow me to introduce Doctor Meredith Blake. She's a professor of mathematical theory and I think you will find her insights are invaluable to our negotiations, particularly with regard to the variables we're discussing. Also, I hear congratulations are in order. Since we're all discreet here, I would like to welcome the next member of the Andraste family to the table."

If his heart had been attached to a yo-yo string, it couldn't have rebounded from the ground to chest and back again with greater alacrity. Meredith met his gaze with a smile, but instead of walking straight to him, she paused to shake hands with each of the attendees and accept their congratulations. Others spoke to him, and he must have nodded and responded correctly, but he never took his attention away Meredith, not when she stopped right in front of the Kachusov attaché.

"I was not aware the grand duke announced an engagement to such a lovely American." The man's hand lingered on Meredith's, but she shrugged.

"We are waiting to the end of the semester. I've been exceptionally busy teaching and am mentoring several doctoral candidates. Couple my academic responsibilities with His Highness' public schedule, and we thought it best to wait. Once his calendar is free, he can take a step back. It's lovely to meet you." And then she was on the move again.

What the hell is she up to?

It was an agonizing three minutes before she'd reached his side. When she tilted her chin up and gave him an expectant look, he obliged her with a kiss to her cheek. Violently aware of their audience, he paused to murmur against her ear. "What are you doing?"

"Making a choice," she replied and slipped out of her jacket. Sebastian helped her and pulled out her chair. Once she was seated, everyone resumed their places and Gencome took a stance directly behind her.

"What choice?" He clasped his hands together and directed the low-whisper to her.

Instead of answering, Meredith glanced at their audience. "Now, gentlemen, please forgive His Highness. I've caught him rather off guard. Surprising him is half the fun, but onto more serious matters...after conversations with Mr. Jacob and Mr. Hannah," she gestured to the Canadian and Australian ambassadors, "as well as my own research, I realized this is more of a trade negotia-tion. You're all looking to make the most equitable arrangements possible which means the biggest question on the table is how to get what each of you wants without giving up things you don't want to lose."

Her gaze fixed on the Kachusov attaché, and he leaned back in his chair. "Indeed, Doctor Blake. That is exactly what we all want, though I doubt any of us would put it so boldly."

"Because you're diplomats and business people. I'm a teacher. I know my students can't answer a question if they don't know what the actual question is."

"Well said." Hopkins, the British Ambassador smiled. "With Dr. Blake's wisdom in mind, gentleman, let's take the time to address what we want and then see who has the power to make it happen."

Pockets of conversation erupted around the room and Meredith glanced at him finally, her nut-brown eyes filled with utter sobriety. "Talk to him," she said quietly. He didn't have to ask who she meant. Like him, the attaché was there for just such an opportunity and all the smoke and mirrors in the room were designed to allow him to liaison directly with the family who wanted his dead.

Sebastian wasn't sure whether to be furious with her or grateful. The last place in the world she should be was exactly where he'd always wanted her—at his side. "Meredith..." Words failed him.

"I know, but the variable of time is not going

to wait for us. Tick tock, make peace, Your Highness."

Catching her hand, he lifted it and kissed her knuckles once before he turned to face Kachusov. By silent agreement, they both rose and moved away from the others. Up close and personal, Mikael Kachusov was an inch shorter than him and he possessed thinning hair on his pate, but he wasn't more than a decade older.

"So, we shall put our cards on the table. That was quite the gamble, bringing the professor." Kachusov half-smirked. "Interesting ploy with the woman."

"Have a little respect for her." Sebastian folded his arms. "She's got more sense than the two of us put together. But she's right, we do need our cards on the table. No more half-truths, innuendo or polite, political discussions."

"Very well." Mikael nodded once. "You and your family should cease any and all efforts within Belaria and go away. We do not want you here."

"Your party doesn't want us here. The royalists do. But you've never bothered to find out what the Andrastes want." He'd been trained for as long as he could remember to avoid direct statements. To couch terms in the expedient, if polite, terms and to avoid committing to any one true course. Suggestion, his father often said, allowed listeners to draw their own conclusions, favorable or not.

The other man studied him with a frown. Reaching into his pocket, he brought out a half-crushed pack of cigarettes. "Do you care if I smoke?"

"Not at all. One good thing about closed door sessions is we can smoke, drink or dance around naked." The last earned a half-smile and Sebastian waited a beat while the other man lit his cigarette. Vidal was nearby, as was Kachusov's man, but both guards kept a discreet distance.

"An odd turn of phrase for a prince," Mikael said on the exhale.

Sebastian shrugged. "I'm an odd kind of prince."

"Are you?" The tip of the man's cigarette flared. "You all seem rather the same to me. A mere accident of birth places you ahead of others."

"The only thing my birth granted me was a life surrounded by bodyguards and a target on my back from families like yours who assume our genetics predispose us to ruling." There was something freeing about addressing this entire topic in blunt form.

"Then perhaps a different life would be more suitable—and safer—for you and your brothers. One well beyond the limelight." Mikael straightened.

Negotiation had been Armand's idea, as he wanted a peaceful settlement. Sebastian, however, was done with being threatened, especially with Meredith sitting less than a half-dozen steps away. "And less thuggish tactics might benefit your family because you realize there are only really two ways to respond to the way you're playing the game."

He had the man's full attention. "That sounds very much like an implied threat."

"Well, then let me restate myself so I'm explicitly clear." Sebastian hardened his tone and his heart. "Mikael, you're a minor functionary in your family. You have no military record and no real pull with your grand-uncle, the colonel. However, what you do have is a family of your own—a wife and children. Your uncle keeps coming after my family because he's worried we're a threat to your political control. The consistent and regular attempts on my family's lives stops or our lack of interest in the throne is going to evaporate."

He paused for a moment to let the man absorb the information. "And I'm going to walk out those doors and announce the return of the Grand Dukes of Andraste to Belaria. We just donated seven million dollars to the health care fund, and another ten million to house orphans and single mothers, a really rampant problem in the declining economy of your nation. Who do you think the people will want? A dictator or a King?"

"You're bluffing."

Any other time, Mikael might have been right. "Why should we bluff? You're going to try to assassinate us no matter what we do, so why shouldn't we satisfy the people? We'll leave it to the people of Belaria to vote. How do you think they'd like it if your family ended up on the wrong side of this issue? It's not like radicals would take offense to your trying to kill us." Sebastian let his smile chill because while he'd never asked for this life, he was through running. "Or try to even the score?"

Mikael put out the cigarette. "It would broker civil war in my country. *My* country."

"Call it mutually assured destruction. You keep bringing this war to my family, we'll bring it to yours." Sebastian glanced over at Meredith where she spoke with an assistant to the British ambassador. "Play the numbers, Mikael. You have lot more to lose and we've been surviving your attempts for a lot longer."

Pivoting, Sebastian let him chew on the threat and returned to the table. Meredith gave him a small smile and reached for his hand. Her fingers were like ice, but he took it gratefully. It took hours, but the conversations begun in earnest with Meredith's arrival finally began to wind down. Seeing his opportunity to withdraw, he leaned over to murmur, "When we're done here—"

She squeezed his hand. "I have a flight to catch." Her reply caught him by surprise. "You have three more days of events, and I have an appointment I need to keep."

He frowned. "What appointment?"

"Your mother invited me for tea." Meredith smiled. "Besides, you have work to do."

Utterly dissatisfied with her response, he made their excuses and escorted her to the door. Once in the hallway, his security team—and apparently hers, since the number present seemed to have doubled in size—fell in around them. He found a quiet corner and rounded on her. "What are you doing here?"

"I told you. I made my choice." Despite her pallor, she wore a smile. "You told me I had the power to decide, so I did. I spoke to your brother. I spoke to your mother, and I spoke to Kate. You needed an opportunity. I wanted to help make it happen. I know what I want and where I want to be. I also know I'm done letting you dictate all the terms." She glanced at her watch. "Now, forgive me, but I do have to go." She kissed him and he dragged her back when she would have walked away.

"You have to leave right now?"

"Actually," Kate interrupted. "She needed to leave fifteen minutes ago. We have a secure window and we're taking it."

Without another word, Meredith gave him another kiss and then she was off with a remarkably tight security formation guarding her. Sebastian stared after her before looking at Vidal. "You knew."

"Of course," he nodded. "But you told me you didn't want to hear it."

"Three days ago, on the yacht." Sebastian glared.

"You didn't change your orders." Vidal grinned. "And she's good for you. Shall we go?"

It was a plot—his whole family and his security were conspiring with Meredith. It infuriated him and, at the same time, filled him a private kind of joy. She'd come for him. Damn right, she was good for him.

~

BY THE END of the second night of official duties, Sebastian was ready to do the assassin's jobs for them. He'd shaken more hands, made small talk in more languages, and drank nearly a cask's worth of wine in small digestible sips along with a permanent headache, and aching hunger to speak to Meredith. Yet, each time he'd called her, she'd taken over the conversation, told him she loved him and gotten off the phone before he managed three sentences.

"Thirty minutes," Vidal reported quietly. "The French ambassador is scheduled to meet with his mistress, and we'll leave with him."

"Excellent." He glanced at the wine glass and avoided the impropriety of checking his watch.

"We have company." Vidal adjusted his stance and Sebastian glanced at the etched mirror. Mikael Kachusov approached and he wasn't alone. The shift rippling through the room was subtle, but unmistakable. The arrival of the colonel, the most senior member of the Kachusov family and the head of their political party—and current senior minister to Belaria—would make such a ripple.

Setting the wine glass down, Sebastian observed their progress from across the room. They were heading straight for him, a fact his security paid close attention to as three members of his detail joined Vidal. The diamond formation closed around Sebastian and, one-by-one, the conversations around the room dragged to a halt.

Catching the Swiss ambassador's eye, Sebastian shook his head once and the man inclined his head. The ambassadorial junket provided the necessary cover and security arrangements to bring Sebastian into the country, but the whole point was to meet with the Kachusov family. To go from attaché to colonel demonstrated a remarkable success.

"Breathe, Vidal," Sebastian advised. "This is what we wanted."

His bodyguard said nothing and remained impassive when Colonel Kachusov stopped in front of him. Cool defiance hardened Kachusov's eyes as they met Sebastian's gaze. "Your Highness."

The two word greeting punctured one layer of tension fisting the room. "Colonel."

"We would speak with you in private. *I* would speak with you in private and with His Highness, Grand Duke Armand." What the request lacked in diplomacy, it made up for in dramatic flair.

"If you would permit us a moment to make arrangements for a private room?" Sebastian didn't look away, but the hush the colonel's arrival caused broke. Vidal didn't move from Sebastian's side and it took only a few minutes until a room was arranged.

An aide handed Sebastian a phone. He paced away from the colonel and waited a beat. Armand answered on the second ring. "He's there?" His brother's automatic awareness of the situation would have surprised him if Sebastian didn't know his security reported to him hourly.

"Yes, and he's ready to talk."

"Is there any possibility this is a trap?" Cool appraisal tempered the emotion in Armand's voice.

"There's always a possibility, however, we're in the Swiss Embassy." Which reduced the chances to a more favorable level.

"Safety first, brother." Armand exhaled a breath. "I wasn't fond of this plan to begin with."

"We dislike the alternative more." When Armand didn't disagree, Sebastian glanced toward the colonel and gestured to the room. At the door, they surrendered their cell phones. Sebastian would call Armand back on the landline.

It was a concession to allow the colonel to enter first—and a show of respect. It mirrored the respect Colonel Kachusov showed when he addressed Sebastian with the honorary 'Your Highness.' Baby steps, perhaps, but in the course of their long-standing feud, it was important.

Aware of the attention on them, Sebastian gave Kachusov the preference of seat choice. The decision acknowledged the colonel's position in his own country, and emphasized Sebastian's graciousness. It also allowed Sebastian to keep his back to the wall. Vidal's tension wouldn't be noticeable to their guests, but Sebastian didn't have to look at his bodyguard to feel the waves of rolling off him.

But it's dangerous... Meredith's voice whispered through his soul and he couldn't find fault with her assessment, however, he had every reason to live. The colonel finally sat, electing a chair near the center and closer to the door. Circling around, Sebastian took the seat opposite him.

They'd both ignored the head of the table and the implication of power inherent to the seat. Side twinging with phantom pain where he'd been stabbed, Sebastian reached forward and punched in the number on conference room phone, speaker on. "Your Highness," he addressed his brother and kept it formal when he answered. "Colonel Kachusov would like a word with us directly."

"Thank you, Sebastian." Neutrality echoed in the words. "Colonel."

Ice would have been warmer than the colonel's expression. "Your Highness, or should I say Imperial Majesty?"

"Your Highness is sufficient for now." Armand's smooth reply did nothing to relieve the strained atmosphere.

"Then let us speak bluntly, Your Highness. When I was in Los Angeles, you assured me your interest in returning to Belaria to sit on a throne did not exist." Tiny white lines tightened around the colonel's mouth and his brow seemed permanently furrowed.

"That was before the airstrike and the latest chatter which met Grand Duchess Alyxandretta's announcement." His brother's response actually surprised Sebastian. Armand, it seemed, was also done playing. "For months, all we have heard from Belaria is a stream of invectives against our family and the purchasing of bounties on our heads."

"You cannot prove the last event came from anyone under my command." Kachusov 's rage was a palpable force in the room. Mikael shifted uncomfortably at the latent hostility in the colonel's voice. "And Belaria does not need pampered royalty to act as our figureheads. We've done fine without your family for decades."

"Yet, you don't deny your complicity. If you are not ready to discuss this matter, Colonel, we can certainly bring it up during my visit next summer." The verbal gauntlet landed in the room like a live grenade with the pin pulled.

The colonel's hand clenched into a fist and the temperature in the room shifted. Vidal was no longer standing by the wall. He'd moved like a ghost to shadow Sebastian.

"Brave words from a man several thousand miles away. Especially since your brother sits here at my mercy."

In for a keg of dynamite, Sebastian tossed the final match. "You don't have mercy in you, Colonel. If you did, you wouldn't have begun your negotiations with the tip of the sword at our throats. As I pointed out to your cousin," Sebastian didn't have to look at Mikael to know he'd blanched at the colonel's reaction. Nor did he dare take his attention off the greatest threat in the room. "You started this private war. We're giving you this single opportunity to end it peaceably."

"Or what?" The colonel slammed to his feet and his fist hit the table. Redness infused his face and his jaw tightened.

Vidal set a digital tablet on the table and slid it across. "Or this."

Silence stretched across the room as the colonel paged through the images. Sebastian had seen them earlier and approved the tactic. They'd gathered photos of every single member of the Kachusov family—at their homes, on the job, and even shots of the newest member, an infant who hadn't yet left the hospital. It made Sebastian sick to his stomach to consider what they were implying, but men like Colonel Kachusov understood no language outside of brutality.

"You wouldn't dare." But, for the first time, Kachusov didn't sound certain.

"Try us," Armand replied into the deadly quiet. "I dare you."

Leaning back and manufacturing a calm he certainly didn't feel, Sebastian dangled the carrot. "Or, I can walk out there and make a statement of support for a democratic Belaria. I can emphasize how invested the Andraste family— and, by extension, the Dagmar Foundation—is to supporting the dream, no royal strings attached."

Knuckles down against the table, the colonel didn't answer immediately. "I need time to consider this."

"Tick tock, Colonel. The offer expires when you walk out the door." Sebastian could practically hear the grim smile in his brother's voice. Any other alternative could give the colonel time to take another shot at them.

Apparently, it was enough to encourage the colonel to retake his chair. "What measure of assurance do we have to ensure you won't change your minds?"

"The exact same amount we have that you won't come at us again." Sebastian shrugged.

"You're suggesting we simply trust one another?" The colonel's tone said he didn't like it.

Neither did Sebastian. "Exactly."

The colonel's gaze went back to the tablet. Sebastian's gut twisted. The other man blinked first, but if he tested them, it would be up to them to make it happen. "I do not believe you would target children."

Sebastian didn't respond. He didn't have to. Silence, in this instance, was a far better tactic. He let all kindness bleed out of him. It dripped the way his blood had when their blade dug into his flesh, nicked his ribs and sliced into his lung. He'd tasted the bubble of death as it choked him and the icy shroud threatened to take him away from everyone and everything he loved. Their actions had compounded his injury to Meredith.

The idea that this man—this one man— could come at them again, could come at her? No. Sebastian would kill him first. The nightmare needed to end. Kachusov met his gaze. Whatever he saw in Sebastian's face must have been enough to sway him. "We will accept your terms, but know, if you cross us...only your blood will satisfy the injury."

"Let us be explicit, as well. My family will continue as it always has. We will devote our time and our resources to helping others and leave your politics to your political parties. We will not endorse you nor will we condemn you. However, if even one drop of Andraste blood is spilled—*one*—then we're coming for you and God help your family because we will not stop until your whole line is exterminated." It wasn't an empty threat. In this, Armand and Sebastian were utterly united. They were done running.

"Mikael." The colonel looked at the attaché. "Summon the press. We will appear together." Uncurling his fist, he extended his hand to Sebastian. "Peace."

It was an armistice at best, with only the promise of mutually assured destruction to hold them to their honor, but it would do. Sebastian rose and took the colonel's hand. "Peace."

THE PRESS CONFERENCE wasn't without its hitches and the Belarian press—or what passed for their press—displayed disappointment in Sebastian's statement that the Andraste family planned to invest financially in Belaria's future, but not personally. The colonel's smug acceptance and the arm he placed around Sebastian's shoulders aggravated Sebastian enough to enjoy puncturing the man's glee by announcing the immediate appointment of two prominent royalists to oversee the distribution of Andraste money in conjunction with executives from the European division of the family's conglomerate.

Still, another twenty-four hours slipped away before he could board a jet with the French ambassador for Charles deGaulle airport. The Andraste jet would be waiting for him at a private landing strip outside of Paris. Nearly thirty-six hours without sleep or a phone call lasting more than ninety seconds with Meredith left him in a sour mood.

As soon as he was on board the jet, he stripped off his tie and threw his jacket onto a chair. Unbuttoning his shirtsleeves, he began rolling them up and looked at the steward. "When we're in the air, I want Meredith on the phone." It was long past time they settled the issue of what the hell she'd been doing.

But it was Vidal, not the steward, who answered. "That won't be possible."

"Why the hell not?" He glared. Vidal played a vital role in pulling off the last several days. Sebastian turned over the coordination and implementation of his security to Vidal. In return, he handled every aspect of the protection detail and it went swimmingly, save for Meredith's surprising appearance and equally abrupt exit.

"We have several hours on the flight and you're exhausted. Since Dr. Blake is currently teaching." Vidal checked his watch. "She will be in her lecture for at least another hour and with her doctoral candidates for the remainder of her day. She wouldn't take your call. Besides, you should get some sleep."

Fatigued or not, Sebastian recognized when he was being handled and saw through Vidal's careful phrasing. "What do you mean, since she wouldn't take my calls anyway?"

Vidal pulled out his own phone and studied the screen. "We will have clearance to take off within thirty minutes, if you wanted to take a shower before you get some sleep."

He wasn't going anywhere. "Vidal, answer my damned question."

After returning the phone to inner pocket of his jacket, Vidal shook his head. "I don't think I will. You have twenty-nine minutes."

"What do you mean, you don't think you will?" *Who the hell was in charge here?* The grit stung his eyes and he ached from head to toe, but he hadn't just put himself through the grueling exercise of the last several days to not reach out to Meredith when it was over.

"Prepare a meal for His Highness." Vidal addressed the steward. "And his pajamas. After we're inflight, he'll retire for the duration. Twenty-seven minutes, sir."

"Get me a cup of coffee and answer my question, Vidal, before I kick you off my plane." Sebastian all but growled and the steward froze, his gaze going from Sebastian to Vidal and back again.

"No coffee. Prepare his meal. Go."

The steward accepted Vidal's word and abandoned him to face to the prince. Folding his arms, Sebastian glared at the man.

"Your Highness, you can try to throw me off the plane, but it would be an embarrassing exercise for both of us. You're exhausted and the last time you spoke to Dr. Blake in this mood, she hung up on you. Save us both the aggravation and get some sleep. We can discuss everything else afterward."

"Since when do you speak to me like this?" It went beyond unusual.

"I've rarely needed to speak to you this way." Vidal gave him a curt nod. "You have twenty-five minutes." When Sebastian didn't move, Vidal closed the distance between them. "Sebastian, get your ass in the shower. Clear your head. Get some sleep. If you talk to Dr. Blake while in this frame of mind, it will end badly for both of you. Particularly since you haven't taken the time to process everything you've done. You've handled the last few days with remarkable aplomb, exceptional fortitude and grace even your brother would envy. That said, I will put you down myself before I let you sabotage the progress you've made with Dr. Blake."

Scrubbing a hand over his face, Sebastian closed his eyes. He was exhausted, all the way to his bones. Vidal was right. He wasn't thinking clearly. Getting to Meredith was an imperative, but if Vidal knew where she was and what she was doing, it meant he'd kept touch with her security. She was safe. He could afford to cooperate. "Fine. I will shower."

"Excellent decision, sir." To his credit, Vidal didn't smile.

At the door to the private bedroom and shower, Sebastian glanced back. "Thank you for your help the last few days. I couldn't have done it without you."

"Yes, sir. I am aware, but you are more than welcome."

Sebastian deserved the rap on his knuckles, but... "Vidal?"

"Sir?"

"Talk to me in that manner again, and I'll loan you to George."

A quick grin creased the man's face. "Twenty-two minutes, sir."

Sebastian didn't even make it to the meal. After showering and changing, he'd buckled into a seat in the private room. As soon as they were airborne, he'd crawled into the bed and collapsed. Six hours into the flight, Vidal woke him with coffee, food and a report.

"What's this?" His eyes ached, and the words seemed to blur on the page.

"It's a detailed analysis of Dr. Blake's current security measures and recommendations for the future. Since her appearance at the conference, we've doubled the number of men assigned to her detail. She's agreed to leave the brownstone in favor of the Ryan Hotel, so we've secured one whole floor. Should she choose to stay on past this semester, we will make other arrangements. We've selected four properties which will meet the security needs of Dr. Blake living individually, but only two will suffice if you elect to stay with her." Vidal took a sip from his coffee. "Further, we've vetted three undercover operatives to rotate through her classes and give us eyes on the campus. It isn't sufficient for long term surveillance."

"What do you mean *if*?" The file went beyond security measures, since it also included a background check. "And when did you run a background check on her?"

"Five years ago, during the conference. Initially, it was rather superficial, but you were only having an affair at that juncture. After you hired Mr. O'Connor, I updated it. I've maintained regular checks since then." Vidal sat his mug down.

"I didn't authorize a background check." A fresh wave of anger flooded him. "If Armand..."

"His Highness did not receive a copy of this report until a few days ago."

Sebastian's blood iced and his temper spiked. "Then why did you do it?"

"Your safety is my job. Your interest in her presented a vulnerability which could have been exploited." It was a reasonable answer.

"Five years ago, maybe. But this—?" Sebastian tapped the report. "This is up to date as of a week ago. You know what? Fine. It's done. Don't do it again." Blowing out a breath, Sebastian glanced around for his phone. "You didn't answer the *if* question."

"Because it is not for me to speculate the outcome." Evasion was not Vidal's usual style.

"I'm too tired to play games. If you have

some objection or piece of information you think I need to know, simply tell me. I'm going to have a difficult enough time with Meredith cutting short every phone call." Weary to his bones, he just wanted to go to her, wrap her in his arms and stay there for the rest of his life. Of course, it might take some convincing to let him back in, even on a part time basis. Hope existed, though. Her appearance in Belaria gave him hope.

Touching a button on the side panel, Vidal invoked the privacy light. It would alert the staff to not step into the main cabin. Clasping his hands together, the man leaned forward. "For the next five minutes, I will speak to you as myself and not your bodyguard, agreed?"

"All right." Sebastian shifted. Vidal only stepped over the line once before —when he'd bodily carried Sebastian from the scene of his assault and told him, in no uncertain terms, he was not allowed to die.

"Very good. You, sir, are an idiot."

"What?"

"I'm not finished." Vidal pinned him with a look. "I've had a front row view to your relationship with Dr. Blake. She's enormously good for you, but you treat her rather shabbily. You appear to be under some delusion that she shouldn't have to choose between you and her career. Perhaps it's too much time in the Americas or a distinct lack of time in France, but ignoring a woman's say so in a relationship is not romantic. It is the act of a madman."

233

Jaw clenched, Sebastian stared at the other man. "Are you quite finished then?"

"No. The initial decision to maintain secrecy was applaudable. She proved time and again capable of withstanding the desire to shout her relationship with you. Quite commendable on her part. Letting five years lapse in uncertain limbo? I'm rather surprised she didn't drop you on your ass sooner."

Sebastian's temper ignited. "It's my job to protect her."

Vidal snorted. "No, sir. It's *my* job to protect her and you. It's your honor to love her. You mistake your devotion for duty and honor for love."

The words bored through to his soul. "What kind of a man would I be if I demanded she give up her life for mine?"

"Don't compound one mistake with another. I know you understand the value of word selection. I never said you should demand, but you could invite. You've made a great many decisions about your relationship without consulting her. Apparently, she's realized this all on her own." Vidal smiled. "Hence, she's begun to make decisions without you."

All the oxygen backed up into Sebastian's lungs and the tension vanished from his jaw. "Meredith ordered the background check."

"No, sir. She requested it."

"Why the hell would she do such a thing?" What had they been up to while he'd negotiated his family's safety? Why would Meredith want a background check done? Admittedly, they were standard practice in the family, particularly for new hires or... His gut clenched. "She met with my mother."

"As well as your cousins, actually. I understand she also has a dinner scheduled with Grand Duchess Alyxandretta and her husband in a week. If you don't introduce His Highness before then, I have it on good authority he's likely to make an appearance at the same dinner." Vidal's tense expression eased with a small smile.

A grin curved the corner of Sebastian's mouth and then his good mood faded nearly as soon as it dawned. "But she's avoiding my phone calls..."

"Her plans do not excuse you from groveling." Vidal rose and checked his watch. "We will be landing within the hour, Your Highness. I took the liberty of ordering a car. What is your destination?"

"Time's up, hmm?" But he couldn't be angry with Vidal, not when he'd given him something to think about. "What time is it in Boston?"

"Late. After nine local time."

Sebastian wanted to rush to her, but then again... "The hotel, but don't tell Dr. Blake I've arrived. Does she have classes tomorrow?"

Vidal didn't blink. "She does."

He had time to do it right. "You're going to hate this idea..."

CHAPTER 13
MEREDITH

He didn't call. The trip he'd taken was over. Along with the hateful looking colonel, he'd done a press conference. Watching the replay of it on her laptop, all she'd seen was the exhaustion in his eyes. The normal deep tan of his skin held a grayish cast. Maybe no one else saw it, but she noticed.

So, he's probably sleeping, which is good. He'll call later. It wasn't as though he hadn't called her at all over the intervening three days. She'd merely not let him have any real say. Dominating those conversations and cutting them short proved to be one of the most difficult tasks she'd ever undertaken. She *wanted* to hear about him and his day, but Kate made a valid point.

His mother made a similar one over the tea they'd shared. All of her children, she'd stated, were raised to lead, making it as natural as breathing for them to make decisions for those around them. The key, according to his mother, was to allow the appearance of control while not ceding actual control.

Frankly, the complexity created quite a bit of a headache.

Royal games were not her forte. Her phone buzzed as Gencome opened the door to the Mackenzie building. Escaping the frosty temperature and stepping inside, she paused to pull off her gloves and dig her phone out. Kate's name flashed at the top of the screen and the message made Meredith smile. *Stay strong. His security checked in. He's fine.*

Having contact with Sebastian's family and friends definitely changed the interminability of the waiting. Today's lecture was her last for the semester. End of semester finals were scheduled for the rest of the week, then she would head to Los Angeles for the holidays. Her security already cleared the trip—her *security*. The thought was extremely odd.

Her boots clicked lightly against the tiled floors. In addition to Gencome, her security detail included the driver who'd brought them over from the hotel and two other men who would be present during her lecture. She'd argued against the number initially, but Vidal explained in crisp terms how every man in his place provided support for other members of her detail. Gencome's sole purpose was her protection. The additional detail would help protect her students.

Stripping off her coat, she tried to organize her thoughts. Overwhelming worry drowned out rational thinking and she really didn't need students already aching to be away for the holidays to scent blood in the water. She set her bag on the desk and headed for the white board.

A handful of students had already trickled in, but her lecture didn't begin for another ten minutes so the majority wouldn't arrive for at least another twelve. Marker in hand, she considered what problem to write. Hell, she couldn't quite recall whether this was the advanced or the basic class—it was an eight in the morning lecture. It must be the freshman and sophomore mathematical theory course.

Still puzzling through the source of the problem, it took her a moment to recognize a problem was already on the board. Backing up a step, she stared at the series of letters strung across like so much gibberish and, above them, an equation–a cipher. The handwriting wasn't hers or Dr. Millner's, who used the lecture hall on the day before she did. A post it was stuck to the side of the board reading *do not erase*.

"Hey, Dr. Blake." The freshman's greeting pulled her attention from the problem. He held out a sheet of paper to her. A second followed him, then a third. She hadn't assigned homework, but every page bore a problem—and a solution.

Torn between the board and the pages, a sudden uptick in the room's volume had her looking at the seats. Nearly every single one was full. Seventy-five students all suddenly deciding to arrive for lecture early was unusual enough. To have them do it on the last week of classes?

Simply unheard of. But still more students were coming in, their boisterousness muting as they crossed into the room. Gencome took a spot right next to her and the other two guards stood between her and the standing room only lecture hall.

"Dr. Blake, is that a cipher problem?" an unfamiliar man with red hair inquired from the front row.

"I think it's change rhythm," another voice shouted.

"Maybe it's game theory."

Once those hardy souls began the speculation, an avalanche of suggestions echoed through the room. Still more than a bit flummoxed, Meredith's gaze zeroed onto the equation on the first sheet of paper. Definitely a cipher, a substitution cipher. The equation worked out to be the number thirteen. Walking over to her desk, she eyed the noisy hall and frowned.

Silence fell.

"Thank you," she told them. "At no point this semester has this type of behavior been acceptable. While I don't have the roster in front of me, I see far more students than are registered for this class. So *my* class will share last week's problem with you. Work on it while I decipher your prank."

Amusement rippled through the hall, and Meredith glanced down at the first sheet of paper. The substitution cipher worked out to—*Once upon a time...?*

The second sheet was another substitution

cipher, only it used the number seven. *There lived the loneliest prince...*

Tears filled her eyes, and she swallowed the lump forming in her throat. Blinking rapidly, she flipped to the third page. The equation worked out to be a five. *...lonely, that is, until he met you...*

On the fourth. *...the woman he wanted to make his princess, but pride, and stubborn determination got in the way.*

On the fifth. *You see, this prince only ever wanted to give you your dreams, it was his privilege and honor to try and make them all come true.*

On the sixth. *He forgot the most important part of making dreams come true...*

There was no seventh piece of paper and Meredith pivoted to face the board. It showed a more complicated cipher than all the others— wait, no it wasn't. A hush filled the room behind her, as if every student held their breath.

It was a Caesar cipher. The solution was three.

The only way to make our dreams come true is if we do it together. Will you marry me, Meredith? Will you make my dream come true?

Digging her nails into her palms, she fought to keep her composure—a battle she lost rapidly. A rustle of movement and the sound of a throat clearing behind her pulled her attention away from the problem. She turned slowly. Sebastian stood in front of her, right in the middle of the lecture hall, then dropped to one knee. In his hand he held a velvet box, opened to reveal the chocolate diamond ring.

The tears she'd held back began to slide down her cheeks. "You wrote a math proposal...?"

He grinned. "All by myself. Well, mostly. I cheated and used your article on substitution theory."

Titters of laughter escaped beyond him. The college students all leaned forward, more than half had their cell phones out. "We're going to be online in minutes." *The whole world would know.*

"That is my plan." Sebastian remained exactly where he was, the ring extended toward her. "I want you, Meredith Amelia Blake, and only you."

"Awww..." one young freshman called out.

"Say yes!" another shouted. In seconds, the others picked up the chant.

He'd put himself out, right there for everyone to see. He'd made himself vulnerable. For her. Swiping away one of her tears, she gave the rowdy students a stern look and they went silent. Glancing back down at Bastian, she went soft everywhere. She wanted to tease him, to give him a little bit of a difficult time, maybe even make him sweat, yet there was no way she could.

Because, beyond everything else, she wanted to hold onto him and never let him go. "Yes," she said and it came out a very rough whisper.

Sebastian's eyes twinkled and his brows climbed. "I'm sorry, I don't think they heard you in the back row."

"No, we didn't!" came the helpful shout.

Meredith started to laugh. "Yes!"

He slid the ring on her finger then scooped

her up and turned them sideways. "Everyone have a good angle?" he asked. A dozen camera flashes blinded her, so she closed her eyes. Then Sebastian kissed her, and the whole world slipped away.

～

THE NEXT FEW days whizzed by at a dizzying pace, but Sebastian never left her side—except for during exams when his presence proved far too distracting for her students. By the time they were safely aboard the plane for Los Angeles, she still couldn't stop touching the ring on her finger.

"You'll be happy to know O'Connor will be back in Boston before the holidays. He's been given clearance to fly." Sebastian told her as she all but fell into the seat next to him.

"I'm glad." She stroked her thumb over the white gold band. "Do you think your brother will like me?"

"Of course he will." Sebastian covered her hand with his and interlocked their fingers. "He's been rather insistent all week that I bring you to see him immediately."

"Do you really have to ask his permission to marry?" It worried her. *What if, after everything, he says no?*

Sebastian didn't appear to share her concern. "It's a formality, Meredith, and only a formality. I will present you to Armand, ask him for permission to marry you, then he will say yes..."

"What if he doesn't?"

"He will. Don't worry."

Anxiety tied her stomach in knots, and she gripped him tighter. "But what if he doesn't? We made such a scene and..."

Sebastian massaged her nape. "He will welcome you to the family. I think there is even a good chance he'll like you even better than he likes me. It's only a formality at this stage, since I told him I was marrying you with or without his approval."

Laughing, she leaned in and pressed a kiss to his cheek. "I don't want you to ever have to choose between your family and me."

"I already have. They are all in a better place now, secure. We've made it as safe as it will ever be." He pulled their joined hands up to his lips and kissed her knuckles. "Now I can be truly selfish." He slid a chocolate diamond bracelet around her wrist.

"Sebastian," she tried to protest.

"Uh-uh." He shook his head. "I know you told me you're not a draped in diamonds kind of woman, but you are mine. It's my privilege to spoil you with gifts. These belong on your gorgeous skin..."

She sighed, but couldn't help petting the bracelet. She'd taken to wearing the necklace, though it had nothing to do with the financial value and everything to do with the man who gave it to her. "Let me guess? You ordered a tiara made out of these?"

His playful grin warmed her. "I can. Would you like a matching tiara?"

"Are you imagining me in the tiara and nothing else?"

"I am now." They both laughed, but Sebastian sobered first. "If you want a tiara, I'll have one made. If you don't, then I won't."

"So, what's our plan?" It took her a moment to realize they'd completed the takeoff somewhere in the middle of their conversation. They were airborne and the only flutters she experienced came from the casual caress of his skin on hers.

"Once we land in Los Angeles, we'll stay in my apartment at Petersburg Tower. Tonight we're having dinner with Armand and Anna. There's a good chance Richard and Kate will be there, that is if Richard has forgiven me for letting you and Kate run all over Europe." The quixotic grin on his face said he didn't really care one way or the other.

"Afterward?" She knew he always made a plan.

"What do you want to do?" The question teased her senses.

"I assumed you'd have some traveling to do—meetings, appearances?" His public life had dictated their time together for so long.

"Perhaps. What about you? Do you want to keep teaching?" The question surprised her.

"I love teaching, but it's not very practical if the students only show up on the off chance the hot prince I married might stop by."

His grin grew smug. "You think I'm hot?"

"Well, isn't that what the papers call you?" Teasing him was almost effortless and fun.

"I don't care about the papers. But, seriously, do you want to still teach?"

"I want to be with you." The answer came so much easier than even she expected. She loved her career, loved the research and working with her students, but, God, she loved Sebastian far more. "If you travel, I want to travel with you. I'm tired of living on separate continents and being in different time zones."

"Then we'll talk about it. We'll make plans that work for us." It was his turn to trace his thumb over her engagement ring. "I've spent the last several years rearranging my life to help achieve what I thought everyone else wanted. The only rearranging I plan to do now is what we decide we want together. You and me. No more assumptions, no more presumptions. We're going to live happily ever after, no matter what."

"Because you said so?"

"No, because *we* said so."

Dammit, she was going to cry again. She blinked rapidly to stem the tears. "I love you, Bastian."

"I know," he grinned. "I'm a prince."

For more royal screw-ups, rebellious hearts, and a prince learning what it *really* means to grow up for love—dive into *Some Like It Easy*, Book 5 of *Going Royal*.

AFTERWORD

It's always a pleasure to share an old favorite with new people. If you enjoyed this, keep an eye out for more old favorites to return after I they get re-edited and updated. Also, if you want to check out more of my stuff, I can't wait to see what you think!

xoxo
Heather

Website:
heatherlong.net
Reader group:
facebook.com/groups/heatherspack

ABOUT HEATHER LONG

I *love* books. Not just a little bit, but a lot. Books were my best friends when I was growing up. Books didn't care if I was new to a town or to a class. They were always there, my trustiest of companions. Until they turned on me and said I had to write them.

I can tell you that my own personal happily ever after included writing books. I've always said that an HEA is a work in progress. It's true in my marriage, my friendships, and in my career. I am constantly nurturing my muse as we dive into new tales, new tropes, new characters and more.

After seventeen years in Texas, we relocated to the Pacific Northwest in search of seasons, new experiences, and new geography. I can't wait to discover what life (and my muse) have in store for me.

Maybe writing was always my destiny and romance my fate. After all, my grandmother wasn't a fan of picture books and used to read me her Harlequin Romance novels.

Follow Heather & Sign up for her newsletter:
www.heatherlong.net
TikTok

ABOUT TRAVIS R COPE

ALSO BY HEATHER LONG

Lure

Blue Ivy Prep

Problem Child

Mad Boys

Party Crashers

Money Shot

Bravo Team Wolf

When Danger Bites

Bitten Under Fire

Cardinal Sins

Kill Song

First Chorus

High Note

Last Word

Chance Monroe

Earth Witches Aren't Easy

Plan Witch from Out of Town

Bad Witch Rising

Fevered Hearts

Marshal of Hel Dorado

Brave are the Lonely

Micah & Mrs. Miller

A Fistful of Dreams

Raising Kane

Wanted: Fevered or Alive

Wild and Fevered

The Quick & The Fevered

A Man Called Wyatt

Heart of the Nebula

Queenmaker

Deal Breaker

Throne Taker

Lone Star Leathernecks

Semper Fi Cowboy

As You Were, Cowboy

Shackled Souls

Succubus Chained

Succubus Unchained

Succubus Blessed

Shackled Souls (Omnibus)

STANDALONES

Kiss of Fate (w/Blake Blessing)

Taste of Karma (w/Blake Blessing)

I'll Be Home... (w/Tate James)

Overexposed (w/Tate James)

Switchboard Duet

Talk to Me

Don't Let Go

Desert Wolf

Snow Wolf

Wolf on Board

Holly Jolly Wolf

Shadow Wolf

His Moonstruck Wolf

Thunder Wolf

Ghost Wolf

Outlaw Wolves

Wolf Unleashed

www.ingramcontent.com/pod-product-compliance
Lightning Source LLC
Chambersburg PA
CBHW010934120626
46552CB00010B/3249